The pot was ove

"You wanna just fold
Luke smiled as he raised the bidding one more
time.

Blake didn't bat an eye. He was sitting on a
full house ace/deuce. The only way Luke was
going to beat that was with a miracle. Looking
up, Blake gazed past his opponent to the bare
window behind him. In the daylight they'd be
able to see the river out there. Tonight there
was nothing but darkness.

And…movement?

Someone was out there.

Blake tipped the corners of his cards again.
Glanced over beyond the archway leading to a
threadbare living room…and saw a woman slip
quietly around the corner from the hall.

He tossed in four one-dollar chips. Noted the
jack and king of spades Luke flipped over,
tossed in his two aces, still facedown, and
asked, "What in hell's she doing here?"

Dear Reader,

Welcome to River Bluff, Texas! There are all kinds of great folks here for you to meet. From cowboys to single moms to entrepreneurs, secret babies, planned babies and another man's baby, you'll get it all in this small Texas town.

The five authors in this series have brought you many, many love stories over the years, but the stories here in River Bluff are a little different. Oh, you'll still have the great characters you won't want to leave behind, the gripping stories and the wealth of emotion. But in River Bluff you also get something new.

Think sisterhood—in a male version! This is a group of five guys, most of whom have known each other all their lives, who are bonded together through life's ups and downs. They get together to play poker every week and they're *friends*.

In the months ahead you'll meet Cole—he's a bit jaded because of a broken marriage, but he's feisty and fun to be around. Then there's Jake. He's the motorcycle-riding bad boy we all want to meet in a dark alley. And Brady Carrick. Brady's been everywhere and done most things, from professional football to professional gambling. Now he wants to come home. Luke, one of my favorites, is just back from military service overseas. He has some hard truths coming his way, but I can't be with him and not love him.

And here, you get to meet Blake. Older than the rest of the Wild Bunch, Blake is the one everyone looks up to. But he has a secret, a burden he must bear, and while he thinks it makes him weak, he's going to find out just how strong he really is.

My sister writers and I hope you'll love the town and the people of River Bluff, Texas, as much as we do!

Tara Taylor Quinn

THE BABY GAMBLE
Tara Taylor Quinn

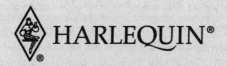

TORONTO • NEW YORK • LONDON
AMSTERDAM • PARIS • SYDNEY • HAMBURG
STOCKHOLM • ATHENS • TOKYO • MILAN • MADRID
PRAGUE • WARSAW • BUDAPEST • AUCKLAND

ISBN-13: 978-0-373-71446-9
ISBN-10:   0-373-71446-7

THE BABY GAMBLE

Printed in U.S.A.

ABOUT THE AUTHOR

Tara's first book was a finalist for the Romance Writers of America's prestigious RITA® Award. Her subsequent work has earned her finalist status for the National Readers' Choice Award and the Holt Medallion, plus another two RITA® Award nominations. A prolific writer, she has more than forty novels and three novellas published. Be sure to look for her latest MIRA Book, *Behind Closed Doors*, available now. To reach Tara, write to her at P.O. Box 133584, Mesa, Arizona 85216 or through her Web site, www.tarataylorquinn.com.

For Tim. Welcome to my world.

PROLOGUE

July 2005

COW MANURE HAD NEVER smelled so sweet, Blake Smith thought, inhaling deeply. Squinting against the bright July morning sun, he glanced down the thin metal steps to the tarmac, scanning the people waiting at the small airport just outside San Antonio.

There weren't many of them.

Four years was a long time.

But a three-and-a-half-year-old child should be easy to spot. He looked for a head covered with blond curls.

Or maybe her hair was brown.

Or maybe *she* was a *he*.

And yet no matter how many possibilities he considered, no small child appeared.

His uncle, then? Alan wouldn't miss this. Not on his life…

What did it mean that Blake couldn't pick out the big frame and ruddy face of the man who'd raised him ever since his parents had been killed in a car accident when he was seven?

Determined to hold on to the sweet anticipation that had sustained him during his eighteen-hour journey from the Middle East back to Texas, Blake renewed his search. Most of all, he sought the face of the woman whose memory had kept him alive these past forty-seven months, two weeks and three days.

The only person he really needed to see right now, after four grueling years of captivity as the hostage of political terrorists.

Annie.

His heart's rhythm settled—and then immediately sped again as he spotted the beautiful face of his beloved wife. At last. With shaky knees, he hurried to meet her.

Annie had come for him.

CHAPTER ONE

October 2007

THE COWBOY PUSHED HIS HAT down low.

Everyone knew that thirty-four-year-old Luke Chisum, of the renowned Circle C Ranch, shifted his hat every time he had a good hand.

Lifting the corners of his two cards just enough to see the pair of aces, Blake dropped his thirty-three-year-old silver dollar on top of them and threw in two one-dollar chips—the mandatory flop bet. His buddy Cole Lawry, seated to his left, gave him a long look.

Cole studied the ten and queen of spades and two of diamonds faceup on the table, took one more look at Blake and folded.

Brady Carrick, ex-Cowboy football player, didn't look at anyone. His face impassive as always, he pushed his cards toward the middle of the table. Brady'd had a hard time of it after an injury had caused him to take early retirement, and he'd headed off to Las Vegas, only returning to River Bluff fifteen months before—a year after Blake had made it home.

The younger man had come home blaming himself for the suicide death of a rodeo cowboy in Vegas—something to do with a wager. Having just met him, Blake had stayed out of most of the conversation revolving around the incident, except to say that Brady shouldn't take the guilt of someone else's mistakes on his own shoulders.

Verne Chandler, a sometimes player with the Wild Bunch, lived in the decrepit, now closed Wild Card Saloon. The older man had moved in to stay after his sister died, leaving the place to her young son. It was there, in the back apartment, that the five-member Wild Bunch—a group of unmarried guys, most of whom had been friends on and off since high school—held their weekly Texas Hold'em games. Hunched over now in the wheelchair he'd taken to a few months before, Verne wasn't looking so good. Though he was only in his early sixties, the wrinkles on his face seemed to be the result of about ninety years of hard living.

River Bluff's male version of the town gossip, Harry Knutson, also tossed in his pair of cards. As did Hap Jones, Luke's foreman and guest for the evening.

Ron Hayward called Blake's bet, just as Blake had known he would. Ron was more of an ass than a poker player, a nice enough guy who didn't know his own weaknesses. Put Ron on a construction site, and he was gifted. Cole, who worked for Ron, could testify to that. But let the owner of Hayward Construction join them at the poker table, and he stood out in a less impressive way. If there was a bet on the table, Ron played—whether he had a worthy hand or not. It made him a waste.

Luke, the dealer of the hand, dropped his army dog tag on top of his cards, added his two dollars to the pot and raised them two. Blake and Ron followed suit. Luke dealt the turn. An ace of spades.

Blake threw in two more chips. And then, when Luke's raise came back to him, threw in another four.

Ron had spent twenty dollars before he folded.

"It's just you and me, buddy," Luke said with a grin, making a show out of dealing the river, the third in the series of deals per hand.

A two of clubs.

Blake tossed in eight bucks. Luke raised him another four. He pushed out another eight. Luke called his eight and raised him four again.

The pot was over a hundred dollars.

Back when Verne's sister had been alive, this run-down and lifeless place had been pristine. Both out front, where saloon customers came in droves, and back here in the apartment, where Jake Chandler, Verne's nephew and the absentee member of the Wild Bunch, had grown up far too quickly.

"You wanna just strip off your shorts and get this over with?" Luke smiled as he raised the bidding one more time.

Blake didn't strip for anyone. Besides, he was sitting on a full house ace-deuce. The only way Luke was going to beat that was with a miracle. A jack and king of spades facedown in front of him.

Luke was no fool. But the chances of Blake sitting on double aces were slim. Glancing up, Blake looked past his opponent to the bare window behind him. In the daylight they'd be able to see the river. Tonight there was nothing but darkness.

And…movement?

Someone was out there.

Luke bounced his dog tag on the table and grinned as it landed on his closest stack of chips. He'd perfected that move eons ago, before most of the guys had left for college. Blake, having come to the Wild Bunch late, invited by his then-brother-in-law, Cole, when he'd married Cole's sister, Annie, had been hearing about this particular talent for years.

Blake tipped the corners of his cards again. Glanced beyond the archway leading to a thread-bare living room, and saw a woman slip quietly around the corner from the hall.

He tossed in four one-dollar chips. Noting the jack and king of spades Luke flipped over, he tossed in his two aces, still facedown, and leaned over to Cole.

"What in hell's she doing here?" His whisper sounded far too angry for the question it pretended to be. If Cole needed to see his sister, he knew enough not to do so anywhere near Blake. That was their agreement.

And since Blake was the only one of the bunch who didn't live in River Bluff, he didn't think it was asking too much of his best friend to keep that agreement. Cole had plenty of time to see his sister when Blake was safely thirty miles away in San Antonio.

"She needs to talk to you."

Blake froze at Cole's response. Then muttered, "She's here to see me?"

There was razzing going on among the others. Blake was aware of Luke good-naturedly stacking up his win. A sore winner. Verne was sipping straight from an open bottle of whiskey. Harry had found an avid listener in Ron, who seemed to have a need to know every gritty detail about whatever drama Harry was sharing, courtesy of his hair-dresser wife.

Blake thought of the Lincoln Continental he had parked outside. Wondering how best to get there.

"Please just hear her out, Blake." Cole's voice was still low, but a note of urgency had crept in. "You know I wouldn't ask you without a good reason."

Blake did know that.

And he couldn't imagine a reason good enough to justify another conversation with the woman he'd once loved more than life.

"I think she's crazy, man." Cole's whisper was clipped. "Going to get herself in a mess of trouble. The only thing I could do was get her to talk to you first."

"You could have given me some warning," he muttered, buying himself some time to figure a way out of there.

Raising an eyebrow, Cole challenged, "Are you saying you'd have come if I'd warned you?"

It was Blake's turn to deal—the cards were on the table.

With one last glance at Cole, however, he stood up. "I'm out."

ANNIE DIDN'T NEED TO witness the exchange between her brother and her ex-husband to know that she was a fool for being there. The expression on Blake's face when he'd noticed her had been enough.

"Cole didn't explain?" she asked, as the man she'd spent two years weeping over came barreling out of the back room.

Blake was not pleased. But he smelled as good as ever. It wasn't just aftershave—though he was wearing the stuff she'd started buying for him when they were first dating—and it wasn't the shampoo or soap. Both of which she'd used for years. It was just him.

He looked damn good, too. Even with the frown and his tight, straight lips. Annie hadn't seen him in almost two years—not since the day she'd met him at the airport.

"I'm sorry. I didn't mean to interrupt. I thought you stopped at eleven. At least Cole said…" Her words trailed off.

She could not respond to this man—not to his anger, and not to his sex appeal. Most particularly not to that.

"We stop when we're ready."

His slacks and polo shirt fit his long, lean body

to perfection. This was his casual attire. More often, she'd seen him in suits.

Or nothing.

Her lips were dry. "Do you need to get back, then? Cole said you were hosting tonight."

His gaze rested on her face for a brief second and then moved away. She felt as if she'd been slapped. "That just means that I bring the food and drinks and pick the game."

"I thought you always played Texas Hold'em."

He stared at her openly. Even small talk didn't seem safe with this man.

"There are lots of ways to play," he said succinctly. "Limit, no limit, tournament…" His voice trailed off, and she knew her time was up.

"You got a minute to talk?"

His eyes narrowed and he studied Annie as if contemplating the aftermath of a particularly bad car accident. You can't stand what you're seeing, but you can't look away, either.

He didn't answer her. But neither did he walk away, and she knew Blake Smith well enough to know that leaving was something he would do without a second thought, if he felt so inclined.

Laughter burst through the archway.

"Can we go outside?" she asked. Darkness might make this easier.

Still silent, Blake followed her out. She couldn't hear his footsteps, but she could feel him behind her—staring holes through her back.

If not for promising her brother she'd talk to

Blake, she'd be the one eager to disappear. But she'd made up her mind on how to proceed with her life, and she couldn't do it without Cole's support.

He'd made it clear he'd give that support only on the condition that she speak with Blake.

"Ask Blake for his help" was actually what her brother had said. But that was a small detail she didn't need to concern herself with. She'd say the words, Blake would walk away, and she could move on to the next step of the rest of her life.

With Cole's support.

"Cole says you're crazy."

Blake's words interrupted Annie's thoughts. Obliterated her confidence in fact. It seemed as if he'd always had the ability to make her doubt herself. It was something she wasn't crazy about in him.

Probably the only thing she wasn't crazy about in him. And it wasn't even his fault.

The rest of it—his long absences, his inability to be there when she needed him—she understood. She just hadn't been able to live with it.

Or him.

"My little brother has always had a problem with exaggeration," she said now.

"So what's this about?"

Right to the point. That was Blake. No "How you been these past two years?" No "You're looking good." She knew better than to even hope to get an "It's good to see you."

It *wasn't* good.

For either of them.

Seeing him hurt. A lot. Far more than she'd expected, and she'd had a glass of wine and a big hug from her best friend, Becky Howard, to prepare herself before she'd set out on tonight's mission.

"I'm going to have a baby."

The startling words got her firmly back on track. She'd identified her goal, and for the first time in her life she felt absolutely, completely sure about the decision she'd made.

"Why do I need to know this?" His words were cold; the tone of his voice spoke volumes.

Blake wasn't just angry, he was hurting, too. Damn Cole for insisting on this. As big as his heart was, sometimes Annie's brother just didn't know when to stop believing in things that could never be.

"The only way Cole would agree to stop trying to talk me out of this was if I asked you to be the father."

THE COOL AIR WAS SUPPOSED to have cleared his mind. But Blake's thoughts were fuzzy, and there was a very loud humming in his brain.

"So…you aren't pregnant?" He could feel a headache coming on.

"Not yet."

There was no reason for him to be relieved at the news. No need to care.

The cords at the base of his neck loosened just a little, and he tried to think.

"But you plan to be."

"I'm determined to have a child, yes."

Blake eyed his ex-wife as well as he could in the darkness. Was Cole right? Had she lost her mind?

Thoughts of the baby she'd lost surfaced. The child that for four long years, Blake had imagined himself raising. Along with the thoughts came the sharp pain that lived in his chest most of the time. While he'd grown somewhat used to the discomfort, its sting was much worse when he thought about Annie suffering from it, too.

"You can't bring back what's been taken from you, Annie."

"I have absolutely no plan to try." Her words were tough enough. The vigor in her tone gave him a hint of the determination she was holding in check.

Life should never have done this to her. She didn't deserve it.

He was to blame.

"I don't want to spend my life alone, Blake. I'm lonely, and I'm missing something important. I want to be a mother, and I believe I can be a good one."

"Of course you'd be a good mother." Blake was scrambling to make sense of all of this—to be a good friend to Cole, and to extricate himself as rapidly as possible. "You more or less became Cole's mother when you were barely thirteen, and he turned out great."

She blinked and looked up at Blake, as if he'd surprised her. Her curly hair was longer than it had been when they were married, longer than it had been when she'd met his flight in San Antonio two years ago.

Had she expected him to tear her to ribbons? To hate her for choosing to stay with the husband she'd married two years after Blake's disappearance when he'd been presumed dead, instead of coming back home with him?

"I've had the magic." Her words were soft, but her gaze was steady as she continued to look him in the eye. He felt as if he'd been kicked when he realized she was speaking of him. "I took the risk and trusted that marrying the love of my life would be enough, and then I crashed so hard I was afraid I wouldn't ever recover."

This was why he couldn't be around her. Couldn't even see her. Did she think he didn't know all this? That he didn't torture himself with the same knowledge every time he thought about her? Four years of captivity had been a cakewalk compared to the pain he had suffered daily since his return home.

"And I've played it safe, too," she continued, as if completely unaware of the hell going on inside of him. "After you, I married a man I'd known all my life—one who'd loved me for most of it. I chose security and reliability over passion. And I not only ended up still just as unhappy, but I hurt someone else horribly. I'll live with that for the rest of my life."

They had that in common.

"I'm not going for strike three, Blake. But that doesn't mean I can't have a family of my own."

She'd clearly given her future a lot of thought. And she made a good point.

Her idea might be crazy, but Annie was not.

"So…will you be the father?" She was good for her word. She'd told Cole she'd pose the question and she had.

"What do you plan to do when I say no?"

"I've already started looking around."

"For a sperm bank?" Was that how these things were done?

Annie's head dropped—something that had happened a little too often during their time together. And always when she was suffering from the low self-esteem, the doubts, that had plagued her since her father's death.

But what did her father's suicide have to do with this?

"I can't take that chance," she said, quietly but firmly. And then she looked up. "I'll have to know the man," she said adamantly. "I'll have to know that he's emotionally strong."

Blake could understand. He really could. But… "Annie, you can't just go up to a man on the street and ask him to give you a baby. In the first place, you have to think of him, too. What role is he going to play? And do you want the father of your child to be someone who'd be willing to father a child and then walk away?"

The problems with her plan were numerous, coming at him from all directions.

"Are you planning to use artificial insemination?"

he asked before she could respond to his first set of objections. "Because I don't think you're the kind of woman to have casual sex with a man and then walk away. And even if you were, you'd have to hope he either had a very understanding significant other or that he was completely unattached. And that he would remain unattached for the length of time it took to get you pregnant. Because your chances of getting pregnant on one try are pretty slim…

"And what if he does have a wife or partner? What if she decides she wants to have a part in raising his child?"

Annie shaking her head brought him back to reality. This was none of his business.

He didn't care what she did. He hoped she'd be safe. Happy. And that was all.

"I've had a legal contract drawn up that will cover all of those eventualities and more," she said. "I'm going to do this, Blake."

He could see that she was. And that scared him.

He turned to go.

"What should I tell Cole, when he asks me what you said?"

"Tell him I'll think about it."

It wasn't the response he'd wanted to give. He just needed some time—and a good night's sleep—to figure out how to be a friend to Cole and also stay as far away from Annie and her plans as he possibly could.

Maybe, if he was lucky, he'd be able to suggest

a safe, healthy and relatively innocuous replacement for himself.

But one thing was certain. He and Annie were not going to make another baby together.

CHAPTER TWO

THURSDAY MORNING, exactly eight hours after she'd watched Blake get into his seven-year-old Lincoln Continental and drive away, Annie wasn't concentrating well. She'd held on to his uncle's car after Alan Smith—having heard the news that Blake was presumed dead—had had a fatal heart attack. And then she'd sold the trading company the two men had operated together, but she hadn't spent a dime of the proceeds—almost as if some part of her had known, even after she'd married Roger, that Blake was still alive.

And if that was true, if she *had* known, marrying Roger had been the act of a coward. And a weak, disloyal thing to do.

At least she'd had a nest egg—and a car—to give Blake upon his difficult return home two years before.

Now, she wished he'd sell the damn car. Let go of the past. Let go, period.

Blake was the most controlled and logical human being she'd ever met. Just once, she'd like to hear him yell at the top of his lungs.

Positively Alive! Annie looked at the column heading on her computer screen. Her focus had to be on the future and not on a past she couldn't change. And for the next hour, her future contained the column that was promised to the *River's Run* editor and publisher, Mike Bailey, her boss, by ten o'clock.

The readers of *River's Run,* the local five-days-a-week newspaper, would be expecting Annie's weekly tidbit on living positively. She could talk about taking control of your life, about being a doer rather than a victim. She could even tell them about the baby she was going to have.

She could talk about Wade Barstow, the richest man in town, and the generous contributions he'd made to the schools and the city and the local churches. Wade was generous when it came to money. Annie just wasn't sure his motives were philanthropic.

She could talk about what a gift the beautiful weather was.

Yet what she really felt like doing was crying. Which made no sense at all. Nothing had changed in the past twenty-four hours. She'd been twice divorced then, too. No one close to her was sick or dying.

Annie settled her laptop more firmly on the card table that served as her kitchen table, coffee table and desk, reminding herself of all the reasons she was glad to be alive.

Yet all she could think about was Blake. The

things she'd had and lost. The things she'd wanted and never gotten.

Standing abruptly, she shut down her computer, closed the lid and put it in its case. She made a quick trip to her bedroom, past the twin bed and trunk that took up too little space in the room, and into the adjoining bath to fasten her hair back with barrettes and freshen her lipstick. Then she returned to the kitchen, stopping for only a brief moment to survey the bedroom next to hers, with its new carpet and the hand-carved, Tim Lawry–original crib. A changing table and matching rocker in wood, and the wallpaper she'd bought the previous weekend… The nursery was coming along nicely.

As soon as it was done, she'd start on the rest of the house.

For now, however, she was going to the office. And she'd pray that she found some positive inspiration when she got there.

SHE'D TALKED ABOUT the importance of honesty and self-awareness, and Mike thought it was the best column she'd ever written. Annie didn't know about that—she wrote three columns a week, and also covered most of the small town's more newsworthy stories—but she felt one hundred percent better than she had earlier that morning.

Strapping the laptop case to the rack on her bicycle outside the *River's Run* offices on Main Street, she threw one leg over the bike and started off. Becky Howard, the high-school nurse, only had half an hour for lunch, and Annie was eager to talk to her best friend—to tell her about the previous night's encounter with Blake.

Everyone in River Bluff knew about Annie's past—her fairy-tale marriage to Blake Smith, his disappearance and declared death, her second marriage and then Blake's homecoming. She'd felt as if the eyes of the world had been upon her the morning she'd gone to meet Blake's plane. People she'd never spoken to in her life had been waiting to see if she'd stay with Roger or return to Blake. And most—with the exception of Roger's friends and loved ones— couldn't help being a little saddened by her choice.

Many had told her so, thinking she'd turned her back on true love.

Only Becky had understood. And maybe Blake.

Her mother certainly hadn't. But then, June Lawry and Annie hadn't seen eye to eye since Annie had been in junior high.

River Bluff High School was on the outskirts of town, part of a complex that also housed the junior high where Annie had been the day her father had shot himself. Avoiding that part of the school grounds where she'd heard the news, she unlatched her laptop from the bike carrier—theft happened even in River Bluff, if you made the temptation great enough—and left her yellow ten-speed unlocked in the rack with a dozen other bikes.

Becky wasn't in her office.

Nor was she in the lunchroom. Or the teachers' lounge.

Fifteen minutes of her friend's lunch break had already passed and Annie had no idea where to look next.

"Hi, Ms. Kincaid."

"How you doing, Katie? Tell your mom thanks for the apple jelly. It was great!"

"I will." The blond senior smiled as she continued on her way down the hall, and then turned. "You wouldn't happen to know where Shane is, would you?"

"I hope in class," Annie said, wondering why the girl would be asking about a boy who was three years younger than she was. Wondering, too, why the girls here all thought it was okay to expose themselves in those extremely low cut pants and two-inch shirts.

And when had Katie gotten that butterfly tattooed on her lower back? Her mother must have shed some tears over that.

SHE FOUND BECKY IN HER silver Tahoe—sitting alone in a parking lot filled to capacity with cars, but no people.

One look at the tears on her friend's face and Annie opened the passenger door without waiting for an invitation.

"What's wrong?" she asked, sliding in and closing her door with a quick jerk on the inside handle.

"Oh." Becky gave her an embarrassed glance, sniffled and made a swipe at her face, as if she could erase the evidence of her distress. "Hi. I didn't know you were here."

Annie frowned. If someone had hurt her friend…

"I've been thinking about you all morning," Becky said, her attempt at a smile weak at best. "Tell me how it went."

As far as Annie was concerned, her trials and tribulations were a low priority at the moment.

"What's wrong, Bec?" Her friend's auburn curls had pulled loose from the ponytail she always wore when she worked.

Naturally curly hair was only one of the many things Annie and Becky Howard had in common.

"I just sent a student to a hospital in San Antonio for tests."

Annie's skin grew cold. "Is it serious?"

"I think he has an ulcer. He's been vomiting blood."

Staring at Becky's bent head, Annie tried to read her friend's mind. Certainly a sixteen- or seventeen-year-old with an ulcer had a serious problem. It would be indicative of some pretty severe emotional struggles, if nothing else. But it was still treatable.

She'd watched Becky work a car accident one time on the side of the road; they'd passed just after the crash occurred, and had stopped to see if they could help. One young man had died, but Becky had saved the life of another.

And she'd never shed a tear.

"So what's really wrong?"

Becky looked up, and her eyes filled with fresh tears.

"I just saw Luke coming out of the grocery store. I wanted yogurt for lunch."

Damn. "They don't have yogurt in the cafeteria?"

"Not strawberry banana."

"Did he say something?" Annie asked gently. Becky was the most loving person she'd ever known. Luke's leaving town to join the army sixteen years before, walking out on Becky and their love affair so abruptly, without a backward glance, had nearly destroyed her friend. And just as abruptly, a month ago, he'd returned to town.

"No…" Becky's voice trailed off. "I didn't give him a chance."

"Do you think he saw you?"

"He looked straight at me." Becky's lips trembled. "I can't believe this, Annie," she said with a deep shudder. "I got over Luke Chisum years ago. I want nothing to do with him. And still, seeing him out of the blue like that, I turn to mush."

Annie wanted to believe that a girl *could* get over her first love. Even if he had been the knight-in-shining-armor kind.

"It's just that, seeing him up close…"

Remembering her first sight of Blake, two years before, when he'd stepped off that plane, Annie felt her own throat tighten. "Aw, hon." She hated seeing her friend hurt. "I'm sorry."

Becky sniffled and blew her nose.

"It gets easier," Annie murmured, though she wasn't as certain of that this morning as she might have been the day before.

Becky nodded. "It has to, doesn't it?"

Annie sure as hell hoped so.

"He's got this tiny scar by his left eye…."

"From the helicopter crash?"

"I don't know, but probably. It's still a little pink, so it has to be fresh." She paused, glanced out the windshield and then looked back at Annie, her eyes filled with tenderness—and pain. "I just can't stop thinking about him over there in Iraq, about all the things we hear about that place. About the crash. What if he'd been taken hostage?"

Grabbing her friend's hand, Annie gave it a squeeze. "Don't let those demons get you, Bec," she said. "You'll drive yourself crazy."

And Annie, more than most, knew the truth of this. "Cole says he's fine," she continued. "Still the same old joking-around Luke."

"All that joking covers a lot."

Annie didn't doubt it. Luke Chisum had been home only a month and already he was taking his father to therapy, doing everything he could to make his mother's life easier, doing his share at the family ranch—in spite of an older brother who treated him with open hostility every chance he got.

"Still, other than some color blindness due to damage to the optic nerve, he seems to have completely recovered."

Becky tried to smile. And failed. "Do you know how long he was at Walter Reed?"

The amount of time he'd spent in the veterans' hospital would give a medical professional like Becky a fairly good idea of the extent of Luke's injuries.

"I don't." Annie hesitated, thought and then continued, "I know that he got a medical discharge, though. With his vision the way it is, he wouldn't meet army regulations."

"I wondered," Becky said, and looked at Annie again. "He's back for good, isn't he?"

"Cole thinks so."

"Think he'll let me just go on not speaking to him for the rest of our lives?" Becky's attempt at a smile was a bit more successful that time.

Annie tilted her head, trying to assess her friend. "You want him to?"

"Depends on the day."

Annie understood that completely.

"SO TELL ME ABOUT LAST night." Becky was calm once more, her capable, reliable self as she turned the tables on Annie.

Glancing at her watch, Annie asked, "Don't you have to get back?"

"I'm working at the clinic this afternoon. I have another hour before I have to be there."

"Did you get that yogurt you were after?"

Becky grimaced and shook her head. "I was on my way in when I saw Luke. So I turned around and came back here."

Annie had figured as much. "Why don't we load the bike up and go to my place? I'll make us some tuna salad and we can talk."

SHE ADDED PICKLES and onion to the tuna, put a plate of thin wheat crackers on the table, and they nibbled as Annie relayed, almost word for word, the scene between her and Blake the night before.

"Do you think I'm crazy?" she asked her friend as her story came to its end.

"Not at all." Becky didn't hesitate. "The world has changed so much in the past five years," she said. "Not only has it become common for women to assume challenging roles in the workplace, we're learning that we have all kinds of personal strengths we didn't realize we had. Society, as a whole, is also more focused on getting the most out of life. Going after what we want. And you're a product of that."

"I live in a tiny town in Texas, in the middle of nowhere," Annie reminded her.

"With the Internet, no place is in the middle of nowhere anymore."

Annie knew she'd needed to talk to Becky. Her friend had always had a way of making sense of the world, most particularly when Annie couldn't seem to do so herself.

"I wrote in my column this morning about being honest," she said, thinking aloud. "And the one thought I kept coming back to was how badly I want this baby. I mean, I get a little scared sometimes, when I think of raising a child all alone, but mostly I just feel peaceful about the idea. I'm so sure this is the right step for me."

"Not that it matters," Becky said, laying a hand on top of Annie's, "but I think so, too."

"You do?"

"Yeah."

"You've never said so."

"I didn't want to encourage you, in case you weren't sure."

"So what makes you say so now?"

"It meant so much to you that you were willing to risk the pain of seeing Blake again—even knowing that he'd say no."

Annie was tempted to say nothing. But this was Becky.

"He didn't actually say no yet." It meant nothing. "I think he has to at least give the appearance of considering the idea, because of his friendship with Cole."

Damn Cole for putting her—and Blake—in this position. As much as she adored her younger brother, there were times when his stubborn refusal to accept that she and Blake were over grated on her nerves.

Becky was staring at her. "Blake didn't say no?"

"Not yet. But he will."

"What did he say?" The interest in Becky's eyes scared Annie. As if there was something there…

"That he'd think about it. Like I said, he has to, because he's still Cole's friend." She wanted to make that point abundantly clear.

"Did he say when he'd let you know?"

"No. He'll probably just give Cole a call. I'm half expecting to hear from my interfering brother any minute now."

"What if he doesn't say no?"

Annie's heart nearly stopped, and then her breathing followed suit. Both started again raggedly.

"He's going to say no." That's all there was to it. "I've got my first interview with a prospective donor next week in Houston."

"Who with?" Becky's surprise seemed to distract her—which was a good thing as far as Annie was concerned. "Why didn't you tell me?"

"I just set it up this morning," she replied. "He's a communications professor, a friend of someone I worked with at the station in San Antonio when I was married to Blake. He's widowed, fifty-seven, has two grown kids and a woman friend who is in complete support of the 'project,' as he called it."

"He called your baby a project?"

Annie hadn't been thrilled with that, either.

"HEY, DO YOU KNOW WHY Katie Hollister would be looking for Shane?" Annie asked as she and Becky tidied up after the lunch they'd barely touched.

"They hardly know each other," Becky said, shaking her head. "She's a senior, and Shane just started high school."

"That's what I thought." The Hollisters lived across the street from the three-bedroom ranch home Annie and Roger had bought when they got married.

Annie repeated the conversation she'd had with her young neighbor at school earlier that day.

"She's seen Shane over here often enough with me," Becky said. The women frequently had Sunday dinner together.

Becky, who was the daughter of River Bluff's sheriff, had been raised by her father's exceedingly strict mother, and she was sometimes as eager as Annie to escape family get-togethers.

"Guess that's why she'd assume you'd know," Becky was saying now, but she was frowning, and she seemed to be thinking about far more than that.

"Could also be that we live in the same town we grew up in and everyone knows we're best friends," Annie teased, wiping crumbs off the counter. "So what's up? Why would a popular girl like Katie be looking for a guy three years younger than she is?"

"I have no idea, but I intend to find out."

"If it's a romantic thing, I doubt your son is going to open up to his mother about it," Annie observed.

"Of course it isn't romantic." Becky's voice became more adamant with every word. "He's barely fifteen years old," she added, as if that explained it all. "Girls like Katie Hollister go for football captains and college guys, not younger boys."

Unless the boy in question had great muscles and a gorgeous face like Shane Howard's? Annie sure hoped not. The last thing Becky needed right now was problems with her son. And the last thing Shane needed was to be led off track by hormones and a slightly wild older woman. He was a good kid, with decent grades and a plan for his future.

ANNIE FOLLOWED BECKY back out to the car to retrieve her bike.

"You call me the second you hear from Blake," her friend demanded, closing the back of the Tahoe.

"I'm not going to hear from him."

Becky's expression was firm as she stood there, shoulders back. "You might, Annie. You need to be prepared for that."

No, she didn't. But she'd be fine, either way.

"Have you thought about what you'll do if he says yes?"

"He's not going to say yes."

Becky's keys dangled from her fingers as she put her hands on her hips. "I hope you're right."

Annie knew what Becky was trying to do here. She wanted Annie's eyes wide open so she wouldn't be blindsided—and get hurt. "Remember last New Year's Eve?" she asked.

Shane had been at a party hosted by the town council for all the local teens. They'd been locked in at the high school. And Becky and Annie had spent the night in Annie's newly empty house, grilling steaks, drinking wine and thinking positively about the life ahead of them.

"Yeah," Becky said slowly.

"We said we were going to keep our thoughts on the things we want. And that we weren't going to worry about things that haven't happened—most particularly, when they probably *won't* happen."

"We were talking about getting cancer or being hurt or…"

"Blake saying yes to fathering my child."

"Oh, honey, bless your heart," Becky said, as she saw the tears in her eyes.

"He did that once, you know." Annie's voice was little more than a whisper.

And then he'd left the country on business, even though Annie had begged him not to go, and she'd miscarried, and he hadn't come back….

CHAPTER THREE

"THANKS FOR SEEING ME, Mr. Smith. I brought a copy of my résumé for you." The twentysomething, smartly dressed young man seemed to have enough energy for the two of them Friday morning. A damn good thing, as Blake had slept little in the two nights since his ex-wife's invasion of his life.

"I'm sorry if Marta gave you the impression I'm hiring," he said now, taking the linen-covered portfolio he'd just been handed. "I'm a one-man show in here and my secretary's got all of the administrative duties covered."

"She did relay that information," Colin Warner said, his slightly spiky hair bringing an inward grin to Blake's rather bleak state of mind. He tried to picture any of the Wild Bunch showing up at the poker table with similar hair—or any kind of styling, for that matter. "I'd still like to speak with you, if I may."

Better that, Blake told himself, than think about friendships and impossible requests from determined women.

"Marta said you have a proposition for me."

"I do—an investment."

Eyes narrowed, Blake shifted in his chair. "Go on."

"Just not your usual sort."

"How do you know my usual sort?" If he had one, he didn't know about it.

"Everyone has his or her own unique signature, a personal collection of habitual actions, with which he leaves an individual mark on the space he occupies."

In theory, Blake agreed.

"You, for example, tend to buy based on three things—global use, word of mouth and thorough financial analysis. You've been in business for two years, you've dealt mainly in real estate and insurance, though there's the half interest in Cowboy Bob's...."

A steak franchise that one of his uncle's former clients had brought his way.

"Land, peace of mind and food—things everyone needs. You buy only when you're approached, and you've made a profit on every single transaction to date."

Did this kid know Blake was set to clear close to a quarter of a million this year, too?

Did he know what kind of toilet paper Blake used?

Because he prided himself on giving everyone a shot—and was in need of a diversion—Blake continued to listen.

"What I have to offer you fits only one of those three models."

"What do you have to sell?" Blake asked, wishing he'd taken a moment to look over Warner's résumé. The kid was entertaining, if nothing else.

"Me."

"You." He'd just said he wasn't hiring. The income he'd earned this past year could just as easily be cut in half if he made a bad choice. But Blake could take that risk when he had only himself to consider.

And Marta. While most of Smith Investment's profit went back into the business, Blake could afford one decent salary.

One. Not two.

"I've got a bachelor of business administration in finance from Texas A & M, with a specialization in investment analysis and valuation."

Blake wasn't surprised.

"In two years you've more than doubled your initial investment, Mr. Smith," the younger man said, leaning forward, almost as if his eagerness might launch him across Blake's desk. "You're ripe for growth. Yet you wait for people to come to you with opportunities."

Blake didn't like the way that sounded. He chose to do business as he did for two reasons, he reminded himself. First, because he was still, after four years locked up in a hole, rediscovering his financial legs. A lot had happened with the Internet, and with the economy, in the time he'd been gone. And second, with his and his uncle's old business contacts, there were enough opportunities to keep him busy.

"I have no money to invest, but I have the skills and interest required to seek out potential buys—to do all the tedious research needed to put you in the driver's seat on any deal you choose to pursue," Colin continued, apparently undeterred by Blake's silence.

Which kind of impressed Blake. Or maybe he was just grateful to the kid for interrupting his life. A life that had suited him fine until he'd gone to play Texas Hold'em the other night.

"I can't afford another salary yet." He figured Colin already knew that—it wasn't hard to figure out if he'd followed Blake's investments and knew the profit margin on them. "I started with a chunk of money I inherited, and I've done well enough, but I've not been at this long enough to be certain that my good luck will continue."

"Your decisions rest on more than luck, Mr. Smith. That much is obvious." Colin's sincerity was beginning to verge on hero worship.

And Blake, in his current state, wasn't entirely immune to that.

"Luck only works a percentage of the time," Colin added. "What I'm proposing is this. You take me on as part of the company, providing the usual benefits, which you can get at a decent cost because you own part of a growing insurance company. And I'll work strictly on a commission basis. Any deal I find for us that you close, I get five percent of the profit."

Intent now, Blake studied the young man. "How do you live, in the meantime?"

"I've got about a year's worth of living expenses saved. If I don't do something for us in a year's time, I'm not as good at this as I think I am, and I need to move on."

"Do you smoke?"

"No."

"Have any preexisting conditions I need to be aware of?"

"No."

It was just going to cost him the insurance premium on a healthy, fit, low-risk male.

"You'd also have to be willing to handle any day-to-day follow-up and phone calls for me, if I need to be out of the office for any reason."

Blake hadn't had a vacation since his return home. And certainly not in the four years before that.

"Does this mean you're investing in me, sir?"

"You a Cowboys fan?"

"Isn't everyone?"

"Ever heard of Brady Carrick?"

"The wide receiver who busted his knee, had to retire and ended up losing a fortune in Vegas?"

"That's the one. He's recently moved back to the area and is looking for a horse."

"You know him?"

"He's a friend."

"And you want me to find him a horse?"

"Brady's family owns the Cross Fox Ranch in River Bluff. You may have heard of it."

"Can't hardly be from around here and not hear of them, can you? At least not if you watch the news.

They train serious money-making, winning-circle horses. I saw a shoot of the Cross Fox once when I was doing a livestock research analysis for class. They've got this thirty-six-stall stable that looked more elegant than the place I was living." The young man's enthusiasm just didn't quit. "They ship to race-tracks all over the South and Southwest. You want me to find that kind of horse for Brady Carrick?"

"If you think you can."

"So this means I'm hired?"

Blake smiled for the first time that morning. "I guess it does." It might be good to have a permanent diversion around the place, someone to discuss sports with, and to share the obligation of listening to Marta go on about bridge or food or shopping.

"Thanks, Mr. Smith. You won't be sorry."

Maybe not about the acquisition of Colin Warner. But Blake had a feeling he was going to regret, for the rest of his life, the next deal he was planning to close.

"HELLO?" Annie had turned from her laptop but had made herself wait three rings while she cursed herself into steadiness.

"Annie?"

Deflated, she plopped back into the beanbag chair that doubled as couch and all other seating possibilities in her living room. "Hi, Mom."

"I read your column yesterday and really liked it," June Lawry said. "You make good points about honesty and self-awareness."

In spite of all the years in which their ability to communicate had been limited, Annie smiled in response to her mother's praise.

"I'm glad you liked it."

And did you perhaps gain from it?

A few years ago, she wouldn't have had the audacity to hope that her mother might someday be strong enough to take control of her own life.

But today Annie saw the world differently.

"I like all of your columns, honey," her mother said softly, leaving the sentence hanging at the end, as though she could have added more.

Annie let the moment pass, as well. The fewer expectations she had, where her mother was concerned, the fewer disappointments—and the fewer reasons to be upset or feel hurt.

June Lawry was a kind woman with a good heart, and she did her best with what she had. It wasn't her fault that her best had often left Annie's needs unfulfilled.

"Even the agricultural analyses?" Annie teased her now.

"I read them."

"You never told me that."

"You never asked."

Her mother's reply took her right back to those expectations again. Were there other things she'd missed, where June was concerned, simply because she'd failed to look?

A flashback to her fourteenth birthday, home alone caring for a sick twelve-year-old brother while her mother attended a Bible study and social at church, quickly confused Annie's thought process.

"The community church's annual holiday bazaar and toy drive is coming up at the end of next month," her mother was saying, and Annie only half listened, picking up her laptop from the floor beside her. Mention of the church that had taken so much of her mother's focus at a time when Annie— and Cole—had really needed a mom, still put her on edge, even after all these years.

"I have a job that you'd be perfect for, honey, and I was hoping you'd…" June's voice trailed off.

"Sure, Mom." Annie took up the slack—out of habit, and because she couldn't *not*. Just as she hadn't been able to turn her back on the responsibilities that should have been her mother's all those years ago. After Tim Lawry's suicide, the entire family had fallen apart. Unable to handle her personal devastation alone, June Lawry had turned to the church. Which had brought a semblance of peace—but also dependence—to her broken and fearful heart.

In many ways, Annie had, at thirteen, become both mother and father. Despite her own grieving and fearful heart.

But that was long ago. And she'd moved on— they all had.

"What do you need me to do?" she asked now, scrolling through a growing list of potential sperm donors, assembled from responses to the letters she'd sent out.

"I was wondering if you could write a series of human interest articles. We'd have to figure what they'd be about, but the general idea is to raise interest in the bazaar." June's voice gained strength as she continued to outline her idea, and Annie wondered again if there were things she was missing about her mother—changes, perhaps growth she'd been too blind to notice because of her old assumptions.

The idea made her hopeful—and uncomfortable, as well.

BLAKE FOUND HE HAD several things to take care of after Colin Warner's departure on Friday. They just kept popping up, demanding his attention. An e-mail in-box to clean out. A list of to-do items for Marta.

There were stocks to check. A callback to make. And some figures to analyze for Monday's meeting with the potential seller of an apartment complex he was interested in buying and renovating into luxury condominiums. Developers had been making a mint on the practice for years in California.

He'd had Marta collect contractor bids, most of which had come in within the budget he'd projected.

"It's five o'clock, Blake. Mind if I take off? Bob and I have a dinner engagement tonight."

Glancing up at the sharply dressed mother of three teenaged girls, Blake thanked her for her day's work, wished her a good weekend and helped himself to a weak glass of Scotch and water.

Enough to take the edge off, but not enough to tempt him to spend the rest of the evening in a state of forgetfulness—as he'd done a time or two after he'd first opened shop again, two years before.

And then there was no further excuse for procrastinating. The workday was done.

Grabbing his cell phone, Blake hit the last number on his speed dial. For the first time ever.

He switched ears when he heard her answer. But didn't consider hanging up.

"I'd like to stop by, if that's okay," he said shortly.

His request was met with silence. But then she replied, "Stop by River Bluff, thirty miles outside San Antonio—on your way where?"

"Are you going to be home tonight?"

"Yes."

"Do you have plans?"

There was another pause. "I was going to cut wallpaper." And then, as if she was worried he'd feel sorry for her, alone on a Friday night, she added, "Becky's at the game. Shane's playing." And high-school football was a constant in River Bluff, whether you had a kid in school or not.

"May I come over?" If anyone had told him three, four, even five years ago that he'd be asking that question of Annie, he'd have known they were crazy.

These days he wondered if he was.

"I guess."

"Give me an hour."

Blake rang off before she could ask him questions he wasn't prepared to answer over the phone.

Or worse, before she could change her mind. He had to get this done. He couldn't take another day like today.

SHE TRIED TO EAT DINNER but the food stuck in her throat, so she put it outside for the stray cat, instead. The darn thing didn't seem to realize that cats were supposed to be finicky eaters. Scrambled eggs were just fine with her.

But entering a house wasn't. As many times as Annie had tried over the past year to coax the bedraggled thing inside, it continued to refuse her invitations.

She heard Blake's car door and reached for the cat, wishing for something warm to hold. But it darted across the yard and into the Friday evening darkness.

Annie went back inside, locking the kitchen door behind her. Grabbing the glass of wine she'd poured, she slipped on her sandals, pulled down her T-shirt over the low-cut waistband of her jeans, and went to open the front door, flipping on the porch light.

She needed to be on the offensive, but she could handle this. Blake felt honor bound to explain, in person, why he couldn't father her child. She understood.

He was a respectful kind of guy. And this entire strange episode between them was mostly about his relationship with Cole. It had nothing to do with her.

"Hi," she said through the screen door, fumbling

with the lock. If he talked fast, he could be done and gone before she even got it open.

Other than muttering hello, he didn't talk at all. Finally, Annie pushed on the latch, catching her breath as she opened her home to the outside night air—and him.

Blake at any time was hard to ignore. But in a suit he was breathtaking.

And maybe a little intimidating, too. If she'd been susceptible to him emotionally, in any way. Now, however, she was only inclined to get rid of him.

When he turned, waiting for her to lead the way, she headed toward the kitchen. It was the one place where she had more than a single seat to offer.

He took the folding chair she pointed him to. "Your tastes have changed." His voice was more teasing than judgmental—not that Blake had ever been one to point fingers at anyone.

"I wanted the house more than I wanted the furniture," she said, pouring him a glass of the merlot he used to like, and bringing it and her own glass to the table. She didn't plan for them to be there long enough to finish their drinks, but the wine provided them with something socially acceptable to do while they decided not to have a baby together.

It might take a moment or two for her to figure out how to handle Cole's reaction in a way that would be gentle yet firm.

"Roger wanted the furniture worse than he wanted the house," she continued, handing Blake a napkin to put under his glass. "I got the dishes. He got the tools."

She sat.

Blake's gaze settled on her as if he could see inside her just as well as he used to. She wished he wouldn't do that.

"It sounds like it was an amicable parting," he said.

She nodded tentatively. On paper it had been. But privately, in those conversations when they acknowledged that they had to part, there'd been nothing but disappointment. And pain. And guilt. His pain and her guilt. And in the end, her pain, too.

In marrying Roger, who'd been her friend for years, she'd hurt someone she loved. Horribly.

"I heard he left town," Blake said, and Annie stared at him. He was a little too close to her thoughts.

"He has an uncle in Ohio with a farm equipment company. Roger's running the place for him now."

"Does he like it there?"

How would Annie know? She wasn't in the habit of talking to her exes—as Blake was well aware.

"According to his sister, when I ran into her at the post office about six months ago."

"She's still in town?"

"They moved to San Antonio this past summer. Her daughter needed a gifted program…."

"What about his parents?"

"His dad died several years ago, and afterward his mom remarried and moved to Dallas."

And that just about took care of Annie's second marriage—and nearly four years of her life.

"Do you have any regrets?"

No one had asked her that before—not regarding her breakup with Roger. That was a question she'd heard many times, however, after Blake had returned and she'd chosen to honor her current marriage over her first. Most often she'd heard it from Roger.

"He's a good man who'd have given his life for me, and I hurt him," she said simply. "Of course I have regrets."

"You stayed with him."

"I was committed, and I did love him. But he knew I wasn't in love with him."

She didn't realize exactly what she'd just revealed—and to whom—until Blake took a slow sip of his wine, peering at her over the top of the glass.

"From the beginning?" His question, as usual, went straight to the point.

"He knew from the beginning, yes."

Blake didn't say any more, and in spite of all the things left unsaid between them, neither did she.

CHAPTER FOUR

THE WINE WAS GOOD, but Blake sipped slowly.

It would be so easy to let the libation do his work for him. Too easy. And infinitely more difficult to regain his self-control.

He'd been that route. And had managed to haul himself away from the detour before it destroyed him.

But there were others.

"I've given some thought to your request." In fact, pretty much every nonwork thought he'd had in the past forty-eight hours had concerned Annie's request.

She looked about twenty as she sat there, silently awaiting his response. Instead of filling out with approaching middle age, she was thinner now, her belly flatter—and more tanned, he saw from the sliver of skin showing between the bottom of her shirt and the low-cut top of her jeans.

His gaze settled there, finding momentary escape. But then that belly was a reminder of other things, too.

"What happened?" His dry throat made speech difficult.

Annie was frowning. "What do you mean? What happened when?"

There was a time when she'd known what he was thinking, sometimes even before he did. Back then they'd talked in code, their own particular language of half-spoken thoughts understood only by the two of them.

"With the baby."

He could feel her stiffen. Watched her wineglass tremble as she raised it to her lips.

Our baby, he'd wanted to say.

"The doctor just said it was one of those things."

"One of what things?"

Annie ran her finger around the rim of her glass, not looking at him. "It happens that way sometimes. Could be the egg and sperm didn't fully fertilize, or that the egg wasn't properly embedded in the uterus. Maybe there was some genetic abnormality that would have produced catastrophic results. Miscarriages are common—nature's way of ridding the body of something that wasn't right."

He thought about that. Wondered what could possibly have not been right about a baby between him and Annie. A baby that they'd conceived together in love.

"What are the chances of it happening again?"

How could talking with Annie feel so awkward? And at the same time so natural? Right?

"Slim. I've had all the tests, just for my own peace of mind, and there's absolutely nothing wrong with me—no reason I shouldn't carry a healthy baby full term."

Suddenly, he could feel the tremors starting—behind his knees was always the first place they hit. He had to get out of here. Or at the very least, out of a conversation that was triggering such painful memories.

"Were they able to tell…if it was a boy or a girl?"

Stop, man. Go home.

The interior of his uncle's old Lincoln was beige. With white stitching. After all these years, the smell of the leather still permeated the car. And if he concentrated hard enough he could smell it.

If Blake stood up, he could be driving away in less than a minute.

It took him several seconds to see that Annie was shaking her head, the curls around her temples brushing against her skin. "It was too soon," she said, her voice hushed.

She still hurt. The loss of their child tore at her, undiminished with time. He'd known that, of course, on some level. He just didn't want to think about it. Not unless he couldn't help it. Like all the other things locked away in that cave inside him, numbing him to much of what went on in the outside world. And in his own world, as well.

"I was expecting to see a three-and-a-half-year-old girl when I got off that plane."

What in the hell was he doing? He didn't relive this stuff. This wasn't why he'd come here.

He had a plan. Strict orders to himself.

One of which was to be out of Annie's house within ten minutes.

He'd already disobeyed that order.

Annie sat still, not looking at him.

"She had blond hair, like my mother's," Blake continued. "And curls like yours."

He could feel the anticipation, the sweat down the middle of his back. Could hear the sound of the plane's engines, the landing gear dropping down. And then metal clanking on metal—a cell door closing. Locking him in.

"She took her first step on what I calculated to be October 12." He heard his voice, but wasn't completely sure that it wasn't just in his head. "She said 'Mama' on Christmas Eve—the best Christmas present you could have received."

When he'd imagined all this the first time, he'd been lying naked on a dirty cement floor somewhere in Jordan, shivering with cold. The nudity had been his punishment for refusing to eat until he was granted some kind of contact with the American embassy. By then he'd been imprisoned for eighteen months. Had only known the exact date because one of his guards had taunted him about the Christian holiday.

Blake had grown used to the mental and emotional torture by then. Or at least, he'd become as immune to it as a human being could be, living under such duress for an extended length of time.

They hadn't beaten him. He had no outward scars. And he was thankful for that.

"I used to picture you breast-feeding her," he continued. "I had set feeding times, and I'd sit and picture you, the creamy whiteness of your breasts. The softness in your eyes as you looked at our little girl. The gentle smile on your lips. I'd see her little hand, with her tiny fingernails, cupping you, opening and closing against you. I could hear her suckling. For months, I would wake up in the morning, eager to get to feeding time. And look forward to subsequent feedings throughout the day."

His voice trailed off, but the vision didn't. He was there. Feeling the cold. The hardness. Seeing the rough gray rock of the makeshift cell that a group of extremist insurgents had held him in— U.S. collateral for whatever they might decide to bargain for, following the terrorist attacks in New York City and Washington, D.C.

"She was almost three when she was finally potty trained. Though you gave it your best effort for six months prior to that, she refused to be interested before then. But then, almost overnight, she had it."

And shortly after that his captors had been identified by the Jordanian government. It had taken them another three months to find Blake and the other civilians the group had held hostage.

Blake blinked, his eyes burning, as he relived the first experience of daylight he'd had in nearly four years. He had hardly been able to comprehend the blue skies and sunshine overhead, and the fresh air against his skin had been almost painful.

And so beautiful he'd actually wept as he walked down the path to medical help and a series of debriefing meetings, counseling, hand-holding, more debriefing, exercising, recovering his strength.

And finally, after one brief phone call announcing his arrival, home.

Home.

The hot air surrounding him suddenly cooled, chilling his wet skin. Blake blinked again. Less painfully this time. His eyes came back to his surroundings and focused on the friendly lighting in a kitchen in River Bluff, Texas.

And he saw Annie sitting not two feet away from him, tears streaming down her face.

"I... TELL ME ABOUT IT, Blake. About what happened to you." Dry-eyed now, Annie tried to reconnect with the man she'd once loved with all her heart. He sipped his wine. Acted as if he hadn't just given her more of himself in five minutes than he'd given her during their entire marriage.

He shrugged. "There's not much to tell that you don't already know. I was among a small group of American and British civilians taken captive by a rogue band of bin Laden supporters who hoped to gain his approval by offering him human bargaining tools."

She, and a lot of other people, knew the political part. The official explanation for innocent people losing years of their lives to terrorist factions.

"You were in captivity for four years, Blake. What was it like?"

"Not as bad as it could have been," he said at last. "We were never tortured."

The words hinted at something that remained unsaid, and Annie shivered.

"Holding someone against their will is torture." She dared to push him, which was something she wouldn't have done six years before. She'd begged once. And that had netted her nothing but a husband who was presumed dead, and a miscarriage that had nearly cost her her sanity.

Talk to me, Blake. Her pleas were silent now. *For once in your life, give me even a small bit of all that you hold so deeply inside of you.*

He stood. "I'm sorry to have kept you so long," he said, pushing the folding chair back up to the card table. He set down his glass. "I came to talk to you about this…thing you intend to do."

He'd come to tell her no, and she didn't want to hear it—not right then. Not when her feelings were so raw, her heart still breaking at the thought of her proud, loyal, private-to-the-point-of-breaking-her-heart husband locked away all alone in some cell in the Middle East, imagining their nonexistent child at her breast.

"It's okay."

His brows raised, he glanced down at her. "You've changed your mind?"

"No. I just…"

"In that case, I agree."

As soon as he heard himself say the words, Blake turned around and walked out of Annie's kitchen. Out of her house. And her life.

He drove for an hour, but without leaving River Bluff. Past the Cross Fox Ranch, which was the home of the Carricks, a father-and-son duo who cared deeply for each other while struggling to see who each had become in the time Brady had been gone. Around town, and then out to see Luke Chisum, another of the gang of poker players who had taken him on as one of their own.

Blake had only met Luke the month before. And he figured he'd probably never know the real man behind the happy-faced guy who sat at the table and joked with men he'd known his whole life. Luke hadn't had an easy time of it. Still wasn't, from what little Blake had gathered from things left unsaid at the table. Not only had Luke come home to help his mother care for his father, who'd had a stroke, but there were problems with an older brother, too.

Blake could relate. His homecoming hadn't been the best, either.

The Lincoln found its way past the old bar outside of town where the Wild Bunch played their weekly poker games. It reminded Blake of his life—once filled with love and promise and friendship, and now run-down, a shambles.

He went by Cole's place, too. Sat at the end of the drive of the half-built dream house that his recently divorced friend and ex-brother-in-law was slowly finishing on his own. Blake thought about knocking on the door. Thought about it, but didn't do it.

Instead, with more doubt in his heart than anything else, he somehow found himself back outside the house Annie and her second husband had bought together. Lived in together.

The home she'd gone back to the day she'd picked up Blake from the airport in San Antonio and driven him to the hotel where she'd booked him a room, leaving him with a bank account containing a quarter of a million dollars, keys to his deceased uncle's car, and a hole where his heart had been.

He climbed the steps more slowly this time around. Knocked. And knocked again.

When she didn't answer, he tried the door. It had been latched earlier, but hardly anyone in River Bluff locked their doors. Blake wasn't surprised now when Annie's door swung open.

And he didn't even think twice when he stepped inside, moving slowly through the rooms, listening for any sound that might tell him where he'd find her.

The house gave away nothing. He took in the nearly empty living room and a bedroom-turned-office, with a desk that matched her kitchen table.

Passed a bathroom and moved on down the hallway to another bedroom, not sure what to expect. And that's where he found her. Sitting on the floor in the middle of the most exquisite room he'd ever seen.

Annie might not have done a thing with the rest of her living space, but the room she'd created for the baby she hoped to have could easily have been featured in a magazine.

She glanced up. Met his gaze. Didn't seem all that surprised to see him there, again, uninvited.

"We have to talk." He'd never been much for pretty words, and this time was no different.

Pulling her knees to her chest, Annie wrapped her arms around them and nodded.

He'd come back to tell her that he'd misspoken earlier. That he couldn't father her child. For all the obvious reasons. And for one she would have no way of knowing.

Contrary to what her brother, Cole, thought, Blake didn't fit her criteria. First and foremost, Annie was looking for a man who was emotionally stable. Strong.

And Blake Smith was no such thing.

SHE TRIED TO LOOK AT HIM, to face life head-on. But instead she could only stare at the rainbow mural painted on the wall opposite the hand-carved wooden crib she'd found in a little shop outside of Waco.

"We need to decide how we're going to go about doing this."

Blake's words were so matter-of-fact, so ludicrous, when she considered that they hadn't seen each other in two years, and before that had been separated for four. And were now, with barely a hello, discussing sharing their sperm and eggs.

She wasn't going to sleep with him. She couldn't.

"Have you changed your mind?"

His question made her think.

"Because if you've decided you don't want a baby after all, I'd be—"

"No!" She'd not meant to speak so sharply. "I want the baby."

More than anything. She was completely sure of that.

"You just don't want me to be the father." He'd always been a smart man.

And had managed to miss such key things at the same time.

"I didn't expect you to say yes." Which wasn't quite the same thing. But close enough.

"You have someone else in mind?"

She wanted to lie. Wished she could truthfully say yes. "No."

"But you want to find someone else."

Chin high, she stared up at him. "Don't you want that, too? In all honesty?"

Blake's hesitation made her heart miss a beat. He'd disappeared on her six years ago. And run out again an hour ago.

"You could end up with a man who fit all the criteria and seemed nice, but was rough when it came right down to it…."

Or what? A man who made such exquisite love that he brought tears to her eyes?

Even though he never told her that he loved her.

"And contracts are only as binding as a judge decides they are. Whatever judge is looking at them at the time the parties are in court. This guy might change his mind sometime down the road and sue for parenting rights. He could get a sympathetic judge, and then—"

"Blake." She couldn't sit here and listen to this. "Don't you think I've considered all the pros and cons of such a decision? A hundred times over?"

He knew her. As did everyone else in the tiny town she'd been born and raised in. Annie Kincaid was careful about everything she did.

When he remained silent, staring down at her as if she were a cross between a princess and a toad, she continued. "I don't want you helping me out of guilt."

"I'm not the one who remarried. Or chose husband number two over husband number one."

She deserved that. At least in part. It wasn't anything she hadn't already said to herself at least once a day since his return.

"I'm sorry." He leaned against the doorjamb. "That was unfair and uncalled for."

"Cole's crazy, Blake. And this idea of his was out of line. Just forget I ever asked. I'm going to tell my little brother to mind his own business and then I'll get on with the business of living my own life."

She had no idea why she was holding her breath. She just needed Blake to go.

"I can't forget it."

"Why not?"

"I have no idea."

She couldn't get away from the honesty in his reply. "Okay."

"Okay."

Little fingers of some long forgotten feeling crept through Annie's lower parts. Had they just decided to make a baby? Together?

Flushed with heat, she wanted to jump up, move around, away. And instead, she couldn't do anything but stare at him.

And remember.

Blake's kiss, his taste had always been enough to unhinge her. His arms had offered her a unique mixture of strength and tenderness, providing a sense of safety, but never a feeling of confinement. And when his long legs were wrapped around hers...

"I want to be very clear up front."

Annie glanced up, realizing that Blake had been talking to her. He'd shed his suit jacket sometime between his earlier visit and this one. Loosened his tie.

He looked tired.

And lonely?

"Up front?" she asked, swallowing when the words got stuck in her throat.

"I said I have a couple of stipulations."

So that's what she'd missed. Annie nodded, listening. Trying to focus.

"First, I'm not going to sign any contract that takes away my right to be a father to my own child."

Walls rose, and Annie found it hard to continue

listening; managed to do so only by assuring herself that as soon as he finished talking she was going to tell him that there was no deal.

"I'll sign a contract that gives you custody of the child, that makes you the primary parent, but I want to be known to him or her, and to have visitation rights."

Not as bad as she'd first thought. He was peering over at her, as though waiting for a response. Her nod was jerky at best.

"Second, it must be understood that this agreement in no way initiates any resurrection of a personal relationship between the two of us."

That one was easy. "I agree completely."

Head turned slightly, he gave her that assessing look that had always made her nervous.

"I mean it, Annie."

Like she didn't? "You're the one who pointed out that I stayed with husband number two," she blurted, before she had time to edit her words.

"I'm not a demonstrative guy. Never have been. You need demonstrations of affection. Hand holding and romance and esoteric promises."

I love you would have been nice.

"I hurt you once. And I'll live with the regret for the rest of my life. I can't risk doing that again."

"Blake…" She stood as she prepared to make her point. "You're preaching to the converted here. The feelings I had for you died a long time ago. But even if they hadn't, even if they somehow returned, I would never, ever go back to you."

CHAPTER FIVE

HE DIDN'T FLINCH. Didn't even blink. Which was so Blake. And exactly why Annie knew with certainty that her decision was the right one. He'd just proved her point.

"You're a great person, Blake Smith. One of the very best. But I've done a lot of growing up these past six years. A lot of soul searching. I've engaged in some pretty brutally intense self-examination and I know myself a whole lot better than I did when I married you. My father's suicide, my mother's single-minded dedication to the church as a result, left their marks on me."

Annie looked Blake straight in the eye. It felt good to be telling him this. As if maybe she was helping him, freeing him of any responsibility he might have felt for the failures in their relationship.

"I'm not going to live my life as a victim," she continued, speaking straight from the heart. "I'm not going to blame my parents' choices for any aspect of my own life. What I can do is offer myself understanding and acceptance, and change what I can and work with what I can't.

"I know that I need a lot of love and support. I need words and gestures and all the little moments of love. I need to be able to express my feelings openly and often. That's who I've turned out to be. And I'm okay with that."

He was watching her, his hands in the pockets of his slacks, saying nothing. But the guarded look in his eyes was gentle.

"You, on the other hand," she continued, taking a step closer, "have been shaped by your own life. Your parents dying while you were so young… Being raised by a man who never told you how much he cared about you…"

"He cared."

"I know he did. But Alan never once told you so. And that had an effect on you—you're just like him, Blake. Reticent. Withdrawn, when it comes to anything dealing with emotion."

His "yeah" sounded almost like "so?" Annie's heart fell, though there was no reason for it to have done so. She was only verbalizing the conclusion they'd both reached separately.

"Your way of life makes me feel a little locked up, emotionally."

There. She'd said it. Clearly. Simply.

"I know that," Blake said, but the tone of his voice, or maybe the look in his eyes, left her feeling as if there was more to be said. Or rather, more that *he* wasn't saying.

Her first instinct was to call him on it. And then she gave herself a shake. Blake's thoughts were his own affair. And an affair between the two of them was exactly what they didn't need.

"So those are your stipulations?" Her voice sounded loud, as if she'd blurted the words just to fill a silence.

"I have one more."

Wrapping her arms around her chest, she waited.

"I want this child conceived in the normal fashion."

The tendrils swirled through her stomach again— and lower. Bringing a physical warmth to places down there that hadn't been fully active since the last time she'd made love with her first husband.

Now was the moment to tell him that they didn't have a deal. As soon as he'd finished speaking....

"I'm okay with that," she said instead. And almost melted onto the floor at the impact of that verbal commitment. She was going to make love with Blake Smith again.

An event that, every single time, had been the best, most complete, magical and deepest experience of her life. And, in retrospect, had nearly killed her.

"WHEN?" Sweat drenched the back of Blake's shirt with the effort it took him to remain in the doorway of his ex-wife's beautiful nursery.

She glanced down and then back up, but her gaze skittered away from his. "I don't know." Kicking at a bit of fuzz on the carpet with her bare toe, she suddenly seemed less sure of herself. "As soon as possible, I guess."

"Tonight?"

That got her attention.

Might as well get it over with. And maybe she'd think the shaking in the hands he had tucked in his pockets was the result of pent-up passion.

If he got them on her, it probably would be.

"Oh, um, by as soon as possible, I meant this month as opposed to next," she said, her skin reddening. "I, want to give this the best shot at working first time out, and with the help of my doctor I've been tracking my, uh, ovulation schedule."

Schedules were all in a day's work. Familiar. "Fine, just give me a date and time."

"It's kind of hard to know ahead of time," Annie said, looking so cute with her mixture of maturity and self-conscious embarrassment that it almost hurt him to watch her. "It goes by temperature readings and a couple of other…"

"Do you take it in the morning or at night?"

If she didn't need anything more from him at that moment, he had to get out of there. Seeing her like this, reliving things he'd tried so hard to put out of his mind, was taking a toll. He recognized the signs.

And he had to get home. He had to protect himself from the most debilitating effects of the post-traumatic stress syndrome that he might spend the rest of his life battling.

"In the morning."

"Fine," he said, backing out of the doorway before she could give him any more information than he was equipped to handle at present. "Give me a call when it's time and I'll clear my schedule for that evening."

Catching sight of her slightly bemused, slightly confused expression in his peripheral vision, Blake hurried outside.

ON SATURDAY Becky came over to help with hanging the wallpaper. Most things Annie could do herself, but hanging gluey strips of border was a lot easier when she had someone to hold it for her while she climbed the ladder. And to feed the long sticky strips to her as she positioned them.

They were mounting pastel-colored balloons to match the rainbow mural she'd commissioned, and Becky was making certain that Annie had a perfect match for every strip.

Afterward, they went into San Antonio to do some shopping. Shane had an all-day football practice, to prepare for a playoff game, and the day was too nice to waste.

As was the wine they'd purchased at a local winery on the way home. With a plate of Havarti, bread warm from the oven and apples and pears between them, they sat on big pillows on Annie's living-room floor and toasted their day. Each other. The balmy weather.

And motherhood.

Annie faltered on that one. And Becky, bless her heart, noticed.

"So when are you going to tell me?" the younger woman asked in her quiet yet compelling way.

Annie sipped her wine, thinking about the fact that very soon she might be off the stuff.

Not that she'd ever been *on* it, other than an occasional glass like the one she'd had the other night. Or a binge, once or twice a year, with her best friend. Which usually meant three or four glasses over the course of an evening instead of just one.

"Annie?"

"Tell you what?"

"About Blake."

She'd been trying her hardest not to think about him. Had purposely steered away from his part of town when they'd been in San Antonio. And had issued firm reprimands to herself when she'd realized she was eyeing the backs of tall men everywhere they went.

She'd get it under control. They just had to get the deed done. And then she'd be all right.

Annie glanced over at her friend, unable to understand the wariness in her heart. Becky was her safe place. She trusted Becky with her life. What could Annie possibly have to be afraid of?

"Who told you?" she asked, playing for a little time.

Becky's sweet smile comforted her even while it struck fear in her heart. "No one told me," she said. "It's the fact that you haven't mentioned him once all day that told me."

And that's why Annie was uneasy. Becky knew her too well. Saw too much.

Suddenly, terrified about what else her friend

might see, mostly those things that Annie couldn't recognize herself, she said, "He's going to do it," as nonchalantly as possible.

"What?" Becky tipped her wineglass, catching it just before the red liquid spilled out on the thick beige carpet.

Annie nodded, liking the way the dimmed overhead lights glistened. Or at least appreciating the distraction of them.

Becky's mouth hung open. "What did you say?"

"That I'd call when I'm fertile."

"You're going to do it?"

With a pained smile, Annie twirled her own wineglass between two fingers, staring at it. "Who knows?" she said, looking over and back very quickly. The wine blurred and Annie blinked. "It changes from second to second."

This was Becky. Annie couldn't not be honest with her. Lying wouldn't do her any good, anyway. Becky would see right through her and then pounce on the fact that she'd felt the need to hide behind a less-than-truthful position.

Finally, facing her friend's gaze head-on, Annie said, "I can't think of a better man to father my child, you know?"

Becky sipped slowly, watching her. The plate of food between them lay pretty much forgotten. "He does fit all of your criteria."

Except that he wanted to be a father to her child and not just the gene donor of one.

"And Cole's now completely gung-ho," Annie

added, thinking of the call she'd had from her brother early that morning. He'd just gotten off the phone with Blake, who, as best Annie could tell, had been thoroughly harassed by her well-meaning sibling until he'd obtained the information he'd been after.

The fact that Cole had called Blake and not her rankled. But she didn't have the energy to make an issue of it—inside herself or with Cole.

"He offered to help with the nursery."

"He obviously hasn't been here in a while."

"Not since Roger left. There's no place for him to sit. We either go out or to Mom's. Or to his place. He's doing a great job on the house, and it's kind of fun watching the progress."

"I care about Cole, Ann, but we're not getting off track here."

"There really isn't much else to say," she told her friend, crunching on a wedge of apple that she didn't want.

"You said you'd call him when you're fertile. What does he care when that is?"

Annie couldn't get any words out.

"Annie?" Becky leaned forward until their eyes met. "Isn't he just leaving the goods at the fertility clinic?"

Annie didn't move.

"He's not."

Still staring at her friend, Annie shook her head. Once. Slowly.

"You're going to make love with your ex-husband—a man who, if I remember your description correctly, made you utterly crazy just with the touch of his hand?"

"What? You want to discuss positions or something?" Annie was ashamed of the comment as soon as it was out.

"I want to talk about you." Becky didn't even acknowledge the rudeness. "About your heart, and how you're going to do this without losing yourself again."

"I'm going into it with my eyes fully open," Annie said emphatically, wanting very much to believe that she was right about that. "So the sex part might be good. What's wrong with a little pleasure?"

"Annie Kincaid. This is me you're talking to. I can't believe you didn't tell him to visit the clinic."

"He made the old-fashioned method of conception a condition of his acceptance." There. She'd said it. And the words were as painful, as frightening spoken out loud as they'd been when they were rattling around in her head all night.

"He did."

"Yes," she said, even more sharply. Challenging Becky to make something of it.

When her friend said nothing at all, Annie drained her wineglass.

THEY WERE HALFWAY THROUGH dinner when Annie heard a car door close out front. A common occurrence on this street, which was filled with middle-class families. Especially on a Saturday night.

Tonight she couldn't sit still. The sound reverberated in her brain like a gunshot. A prelude to something to come. A knock on her door? A visitor she didn't want and couldn't handle? Especially not with a glass of wine playing with her emotions.

He was probably halfway up the walk by now. Jumping up, Annie approached the front window from the side, peeking through the sheers without being seen. She knew it wasn't Blake. There would be a car out front of one of her neighbors' homes. Blake had no reason to visit her. Ever.

Except when she called him over to make a baby.

The car out front wasn't a Lincoln Continental. And it wasn't on her side of the street, either. It was a Jeep. And…

"Bec? Didn't you say Shane was at Devin's house, having pizza and watching a movie with some of the guys from the team?"

"Yeah, that's right. They're watching that old Jim Carrey movie, *Me, Myself and Irene.* Shane's seen it before but he thinks it hilarious."

Annie turned from the window, still holding the sheers so she could see out. "He's not at Devin's."

"What?" Glass in hand, Becky joined her at the window and glanced out.

Standing with her best friend, Annie watched as fifteen-year-old Shane Howard, with occasional glances toward Annie's house, leaned back against the Jeep parked in front of Katie Hollister's house, pulled the eighteen-year-old between his spread legs and kissed her full on the lips.

BLAKE AWOKE WITH A START. His bedroom door, which he'd shut and locked with the dead bolt he'd had installed before he'd moved in, had just creaked open. He tried to see through the darkness. Could only make out a thin sliver of light where the door was ajar.

Someone was in the room. He had to get up. Wasn't going to be taken captive lying down again. But his arms and legs wouldn't move. He couldn't turn his head. The covers trapped him and held him hostage. Sweating profusely, Blake struggled to break free, to move at all. He couldn't see anything, couldn't hear anyone. He didn't have much time.

And then…the blow came from nowhere, straight to his chest, a heavy weight crushing him, squeezing the air out of his lungs. He could see the creature. Could make out the large green puss-filled eyes. Could feel the thin, sharp fingers curling into his skin. It was a demon. Rank-smelling breath spewed forth, attacking Blake's nostrils, while matted hair brushed his chin. He couldn't breathe. He was going to die.

Suddenly free, Blake shot up and out of bed. Out of the room, and grabbing his keys and wallet as he ran, out of the house. The Lincoln purred to life and he roared down the driveway, heart pounding as he sucked air into desperate lungs.

The all-night coffee shop was just around the next corner. Blake focused on his destination, on the turn signal and steering wheel and gas pedal. He wasn't wearing any shoes.

By the time he pulled into the parking lot, he

had his breathing under control. Running a hand through his hair, over the T-shirt and sweats he slept in because of occasions such as these, he reached into the backseat for the tennis shoes he'd kept there for two years, since the first visit he'd had from his night stalker. He slipped them on. Tied them. And with shaking hands reached for the door handle.

"Hey, Blake, it's been awhile." Hallie, the forty-something waitress, met him at his usual booth, a pot of decaf in hand.

"Thanks, Hal," he said, taking a sip, the coffee's warmth seeping through him, bringing him back.

Hand on her hip, she looked him over. "Rough one, huh?"

He shrugged. "I've had worse."

"So what brought it on this time?"

Glancing around, Blake focused on a young couple at the back of the room—the only other patrons in the joint. Not many people in this neighborhood needed sustenance at three o'clock on a Monday morning. In another hour, however, the place would be packed with factory workers on their way to their early shifts.

"Just one of those things." He gave the friendly woman the same answer he always provided. And the grateful smile, too.

"You want your usual?" she asked, smiling back, her eyes filled with more than just a professional welcome.

"Please."

And when, ten minutes later, she delivered his scrambled eggs and wheat toast, he thought about asking her to dinner sometime.

But, as always, he didn't.

CHAPTER SIX

ANNIE WAS JUST RIDING away from the *River's Run* office on Monday when Becky pulled around the corner. With one foot on the ground to steady her bike, Annie waited while her friend rolled down the Tahoe's window.

"You got a minute?" Becky asked.

She always had time for her friend, especially when Becky wore that concerned frown. While Becky dropped off her weekly column of health tips to Mike Bailey, Annie threw her pack into the passenger seat of the vehicle and unloaded Becky's bike from the back. Within minutes the two of them were wheeling their way out of town.

"Did you talk to Shane?" That was the first question Annie asked, relaxing for a moment as bits of hair tossed against her forehead in the wind. Becky's son had still been asleep when Annie had talked to her on Sunday.

"He says it was just a joke." Becky didn't sound at all convinced. "He claims that Devin was in the Jeep and that they'd just come from the video store when Katie stopped them and asked for a ride home. Says she had a fight with her boyfriend."

"You don't believe him." Annie slowed her pedaling to stay even with Becky.

With a quick sideways glance, her friend said, "Did you see Devin in that Jeep?"

"No."

"And the kiss didn't look like any dare to me."

Annie hadn't thought so, either. And she was more worried now than she'd been on Saturday evening. If Shane was lying to Becky, they had bigger problems than just an intimate exchange between the young man who was like a nephew to her, and the out-of-control older girl who lived across the street.

"Did you call Danny?"

Danny was Becky's ex-husband.

"No."

"Because Luke's back in town?"

One of Becky's feet slid off its pedal. "Of course not."

Annie sped in front to let a car pass them on the quiet, two-lane country road, and then slowed down until she was beside her again. "Are you sure about that, Bec?" she asked.

When Becky didn't answer, Annie started to worry in earnest. Luke Chisum had broken Becky's heart when they were in high school. It had taken Becky years—and cost her a failed marriage—before she'd been able to find the peace and calm she now showed.

"Be careful, Bec," Annie said, ducking to avoid the branch of a cypress tree.

"Like you're being careful?" Becky's quiet comeback was almost lost on the breeze.

They'd reached a hill and Annie concentrated on using hamstrings, as well as quads, keeping her calves loose as she switched to a lower gear and headed up the slope. In jeans and a sweater, she was dressed for the office—this was not a strenuous bike ride, but she didn't much care.

Riding cleared her mind. Calmed her heart. Which was why she almost never drove the car that was parked in her garage.

And climbing like this, facing the physical challenge head-on, strengthened her. At the moment, she needed all the strength she could get.

She crested the hill, triumphant, and hardly out of breath. Yes. She could do this. Could do anything she set her mind to.

She wasn't a quitter. Didn't buckle or give up. She was…

"How's your temperature?"

Annie's calf cramped. Taking her foot off the pedal, she glided down the opposite side of the hill, giving herself up to the breeze, the freedom. She could fly if she wanted to. And end up someplace else. Another time. Another life?

"Are you going to call Blake?"

Trust Becky to get right to the point, even if Annie didn't acknowledge there was one.

"I don't know."

"Then maybe you shouldn't."

Glancing over at her friend, Annie tried to read

Becky's mind as easily as the other woman read hers. And failed.

"Cole is accepting of this whole plan now and I need his support," she said, curiously worried that Becky might think she shouldn't do this. Which made no sense, because most of the time, Becky agreed about it. "You and he are the only people I have that I can call on a second's notice. I can't afford to lose either of you."

"And Blake meets the criteria, I know," Becky observed. "You know his genetic history. Don't have to worry about someone lying to make a buck."

"Maybe you think it shouldn't matter," Annie replied, half coasting, waving as a friend of her mother's passed, going the opposite direction. "And maybe it shouldn't, but it does."

Becky slowed enough to look at Annie squarely as she said, "I understand that. I think it matters, too, considering the situation."

"Dr. Snow said that the chances of manic depression, or bipolar disorder as they're calling it now, being genetically passed on are about ten percent at the most."

Becky nodded. "Genetic studies are relatively new in the whole psychiatric–bipolar field, but from what I've read, there are some chromosomal indications. However, there also tends to be a need of some kind of environmental trigger."

"Blake and I had genetic counseling when we were married."

"You never told me that."

"I never told anyone." She hadn't wanted anyone to know that she might be as flawed as her father. She'd spent her entire life showing the world a girl, a woman, who fit society's expectations of a perfectly normal, emotionally healthy human being.

"I'm assuming everything came out fine, or you wouldn't even consider him."

"We were a perfect match." At the time, she'd thought the test results had been extra validation of the fact that she and Blake were such a good fit.

As it turned out, those results were the only perfect match between them.

"Of course, you could undergo the same kind of testing with any other candidate."

She could. And go through it several times if she had to.

"I know I can trust Blake."

"Which lessens the risk of the potential sperm donor backing out of the agreement at some future date."

Right. And that was a big consideration.

"And you know him," Becky added. "You know about the things that don't show up on genetic testing."

Still pedaling slowly, they turned onto another long country road, the second leg of the route that would take them back to town. "Think about it, Bec," Annie said, letting go of the handle bars for a moment to sit upright. "The man lived through four years of captivity at the hands of crazy terrorists. He returns home to find the life he'd left completely gone. All of it. His business, his uncle, the kid he'd thought he had, his marriage…"

She had to stop. Catch her breath. Wait for emotion to pass.

"And in just over two years' time, he's built a whole new life for himself out of what assets were left in a bank account, using sheer resolve, determination and emotional strength."

"He's not likely going to be a man who buckles under feelings of desperation, and takes his own life," Becky said. "He's not your father."

Exactly.

"I can't argue with you about any of this," her friend said. "It all makes sense."

"So you think I should do it."

"I think that if you actually sleep with Blake Smith again, you're going to break your own heart, Annie."

"So you think I shouldn't do it." They were climbing another hill. A smaller one. Annie's quads knotted with pain.

"Oh, Ann. This isn't anything I can help with. It's too personal, too you, for my opinion or anyone else's to make a difference. I think that you have to follow your heart. Regardless of what it, or anyone else, tells you."

They'd crested the hill, and with Becky's words ringing in her ears, Annie sailed down the opposite side, scared to death to hear what her heart had to say.

POST-TRAUMATIC stress disorder.

Rubbing tired eyes, Blake lay in bed Monday night, the worn and wrinkled pamphlet held out in front of him.

An anxiety disorder that is triggered by a life-threatening event.

Which narrowed it right down, didn't it? In the privacy of his own mind, the disgruntled thought surfaced.

Who hadn't, at some time in the course of a life, had a life-threatening experience? Anyone who'd ever been in a car accident, or even a bad storm. Millions of women and children were abused every day, but only half of the victims ever developed symptoms of PTSD.

So why him?

Sufferers of PTSD exhibit three basic symptoms. All three must be present for a PTSD diagnosis. They are...

And they were listed. Blake could recite them by heart. Reliving the trauma—oftentimes without warning. And he knew to his detriment that this wasn't merely remembering it, but experiencing it just as if it were happening again. Then there was the need to create a safe environment and stay within it as much as possible. Isolating oneself from things that might trigger a memory of the event. And the onset of symptom one. And last was the natural reaction to the first two. Constantly being on guard. Jumping at the slightest sound.

He could add a few more. Like episodes of sleep

paralysis. Problems with drinking. Conduct disorder. Dependence on drugs. Hell, he could write a book about the damn condition.

What he couldn't seem to do was rid himself of it.

ANNIE LOOKED AT HER CHART. The dates and entries in all columns. The rising curve. Tuesday, October 9.

She had a choice to make.

Now.

She could do nothing. And that would be a choice. Because if she didn't call Blake this month, he'd know she'd changed her mind. Wasn't sure. She'd give him a month to change *his* mind.

Cole would be asking her if she'd seen Blake. As if she had to answer to her little brother about whether or not she'd had sex with her ex-husband.

This whole thing was a mess. Far too complicated.

Which was why she should keep the appointment she had in Houston. And make others. Do interviews. Sign a contract. Visit a clinic. Complete the project.

And get on with her life. Get on with the business of having a baby and making a family. A home.

Making use of her capacity to love fully and completely.

Being the mother she was meant to be.

She was healthy. Strong. She'd survived a missing and presumed dead love of her life. A miscarriage. A tragic return. A failed marriage. She'd survived the suicide of her father, a man she'd adored. The breakdown of a mother she'd relied upon.

The growing up of the little brother she'd cared for with all the intensity of a new mother with her firstborn. And she'd been thirteen at the time. She was a successful and sought-after newspaper reporter. A college graduate. A champion biker.

There was no doubt that Annie Kincaid could take the heat. Go the distance. Move an entire community to think more positively.

But could she make one simple phone call?

She went to the office. Turned in her weekly agricultural column. Wrote up a piece on a Texas state senate political scandal—a vote-tallying discrepancy and the ensuing cover-up—that was going to have far-reaching effects across the state. And another on a family seeking immunity from immigration laws so that their grandmother could remain where she was and die with enough health care to keep her comfortable.

Annie stopped by her mother's house. Picked up some information June had for her on the holiday bazaar coming the next month. Hedged when her mom asked her how she was doing.

And then there was nothing left but the remaining hours in a day that wouldn't end soon enough, or might end far too soon.

Blake had given her his cell phone number.

He'd be at the office at least until five.

At four she picked up her phone. She didn't want

to call him at home, or when he was out. This was basically a business project. She had to call him at work.

Four-fifteen and she'd punched the number once, but hadn't hit Send. Four-thirty and she hit Redial.

By five-thirty, with her phone left on the kitchen counter, she sat at her computer, trying to write. To get a head start on Thursday's column. She couldn't think of a single positive thing to say.

Giving up after almost an hour of nonproductive staring, she took her bike out for a spin around the block. Six times.

And at seven, she was back in the kitchen.

"Blake?" Of course it was him. Who else would answer his phone?

"Yes, Annie. Is it time?"

"Yes."

"Have you had dinner?"

"No, you?"

"No."

"Would you like me to make something?"

"No. I'm not particularly hungry."

"Me, either."

"Shall I just come over, then?"

She gulped. Tried to think. Couldn't form a coherent thought. "Okay."

"I'm on my way."

Which gave her just a little over an hour to pack up and leave.

Or stay and know the exquisite pleasure of lying in Blake Smith's arms once more in this lifetime.

Annie decided to pack.

SHE PULLED OUT a nightgown first. One of the silky ones she'd stuffed in the back of a drawer the day they'd come to tell her that Blake Smith was missing and presumed dead. She meant to reach for underwear—and socks, too. They were in the next drawer.

And then move to the closet for jeans and a sweater. Some shoes.

When that seemed to be too much, she went to the bathroom instead. She'd need toiletries, wherever she was going.

And she'd gather them. Just as soon as she had a second to relax. Hot water always relaxed her.

Annie plugged the tub. Poured in some of the bubble bath she wanted to remember to take with her. Tested the water with her toe and then slowly stepped out of the jeans she'd had on all day. Her shirt followed. And her bra. And then, when the tub was half-full, she slid her panties down past her thighs, feeling exposed and vulnerable.

Vulnerable, alone in her own bathroom.

Where she undressed and bathed every single day of her life.

What was the matter with her? Had she lost her mind? How could she have thought that she could undress herself, give her body to a man's intimacies, and feel nothing?

How could this ever be a "project"? A business arrangement? She'd only ever made love to two men in her life. And both of them after she'd married them.

She'd held the act in such high esteem. And now she thought she could cheapen it all in the name of achieving a hard sought, well-planned and much deserved goal?

Was it immoral, what she'd put in motion? Had she lost sight of reality? Let her issues push her to the point of irrational behavior?

Sinking into the hot soapy water, she took a deep breath. Calmed herself. She should be thinking about where she was going to go.

But she couldn't find enough interest in the topic to focus. To care. As long as she was gone before Blake got there. And stayed gone all night, in case he hung around. She could sleep in her car for all that mattered.

Or maybe she should load up her pack and take the bike for an all-night ride. She could fit in a fleece blanket and sleep out under the stars.

But she didn't really want to ride in the dark.

The moon was out already.

Annie reached for the soap. Drew it slowly up one arm, across her chest and down the other arm. She lathered. And rinsed. And tended to the rest of her body in the same manner.

Would he find her changed? Be disappointed? She'd aged six years since he'd last seen her naked.

Not that he had to see her. She could just get under the covers before he came in. Turn off the lights.

But then he'd join her there, under her blankets.

And she might not ever be able to let him out. Or to crawl under them alone again.

Water splashed as she rose abruptly, reaching for her towel. This wasn't going to work. She couldn't do it.

Rubbing briskly, she was dry and in her nightgown before she had another coherent thought.

She wanted this baby. More than anything. Was ready for it. If she waited too long, she might not be able to conceive. Blake was everything she'd hoped to find in a sperm donor for her child. He was willing. And she was ready.

How could she pass up this opportunity? It was ideal. Safe. It was a chance to touch Blake again, as she'd dreamed of doing every night for years after he'd left. To know again the comfort of being close to him. Breathing with him.

She'd be a fool not to be ready.

She'd never be ready. Not to feel Blake's body slide down on top of hers again, to accommodate his hips and legs between hers, feel him settle there as though he'd been made to fit only her. To look into those serious eyes and see herself reflected, along with the love she'd always found there.

The love he'd never once expressed in words.

Annie needed words. She needed reassurance. She needed demonstration and spontaneity. She needed openness.

She needed a glass of wine.

CHAPTER SEVEN

THE LINCOLN DROVE to her house as though someone else was at the wheel, responsible for getting it to its destination. Blake had only been there twice before, but he made every turn without hesitation.

It was as if he didn't think at all. Couldn't allow himself to make too much of this. He was doing a favor for a friend. Performing a service.

Nothing more.

There couldn't be anything more. Ever.

People in his condition often found it impossible to coexist in a family setting. And always to the detriment of those sharing their lives. Whether he was one of those people, he didn't know. He'd been living alone since his return from the bowels of Jordan. But he'd heard the stories in counseling sessions. Read the pamphlets. Knew the statistics. Knew, too, that it wasn't a risk he was willing to take.

And with that thought in mind, he knocked on his ex-wife's front door.

ANNIE STOOD AT THE DOOR in a gown he'd bought her for their third anniversary. He'd dreamed of that gown during his years in hell. The vision had sustained him through some of the toughest moments of his life. But tonight it hurt to look at her.

"Come in," she said, as if she did this kind of thing every day.

He stepped inside.

"Would you like a glass of wine?"

"Sure." He did his best to lace the response with nonchalance, then added, "Thank you."

And while she went to pour it for him, he stood in her entryway, wondering what he should do next. This wasn't a romantic interlude.

But what about foreplay? Annie would need a little time to warm up to him. She always had.

Those minutes of touching and kissing before lovemaking had been sacred.

Would she want to tonight?

She was already nearly undressed.

Should he proceed to the bedroom? Undress? Hang his slacks and shirt on the back of a chair? Climb under the covers and wait for her?

She hadn't invited him into her bed.

Perhaps she'd prefer to do this on the couch. He looked toward the mostly bare living room. And remembered that there was no couch.

A spare room, then?

"Sorry, it took me a minute to open a new bottle." She was back. Handing him a glass of merlot. Her hair was down, silky and slightly damp, reaching almost to her hips. Longer than he remembered.

He lifted a hand to her head and dropped it again.

Running his fingers through Annie's hair was supposed to lead up to impregnating her. But to Blake, it was more the act of a man cherishing a woman. Loving a woman. Making love to a woman.

He sipped his wine. Held the glass in both hands. Wasn't sure where to look. So he did what he couldn't seem to help doing: he looked straight at her.

"You're as beautiful as ever."

"I'm six years older."

Seemed like a hundred since he'd last held her.

"I'm starting to get wrinkles around my eyes."

"Not that I can see," he told her. "Not that it would matter. You're going to be beautiful at ninety, Annie. I always told you that."

She smiled, glanced away. Blake wondered if he'd seen tears in her eyes. Took a step toward her. And stopped.

"I... What do you want?" he asked, simply because he had no idea how to proceed. How to do her this favor without offending her.

He had no idea of her expectations. Knew only that he wanted to meet them. Whatever they were.

"What do you mean?" she asked, laughing shakily.

"I don't think I know how to do this."

Looking equally lost, Annie just stood there. Saying nothing. Which left the next step up to him. A man who had difficulty just trying to sleep through the night.

"Do you want to talk for a bit?"

"No. I mean, if you want to, okay." Her glass

shook as she raised it to her lips. "But we don't have to on my account."

He couldn't say he was unhappy about that. He wasn't much of a conversationalist at the best of times.

"So, where would you like to go?"

"My… The only place there is to lie down, beside the floor, is my bedroom."

Deciding the floor was out, Blake indicated that she should lead the way. And followed her past the kitchen and down the hall he'd traversed by himself the week before, seeking her out. The night he'd come to tell her he was not going to father her child.

The door to the fairy-tale nursery was shut. As was the one across the way. From the last door, the one at the end of the hall, he could see soft light glowing. She'd prepared for him.

The gown. The lighting.

And the sheets pulled back on a simple twin bed set on a basic metal frame. That yawning welcome was all he could see as he stopped in the doorway to the room where Annie spent her nights. Alone. She'd pulled the sheets back for him. For them. For at least a short while, he would rest his head in Annie's bed.

Blake had no real sense of how long he stood there staring.

But it was long enough for his starved body to grow hard with wanting her. He wanted nothing more out of life than to climb into that bed, take Annie into his arms and never climb out again.

Except he wasn't here to want that.

He was here to do a job. And then leave. The thought didn't lessen the tension in his lower body one whit.

Draining his glass, Blake took a couple of steps into the mostly bare room. Set the goblet on a plastic Parsons table that held an abundantly leafy green plant. Reached for the top button of his shirt.

Focusing on the potted ivy, his gaze following the vine as it curled down around the table to trail along the floor, he undid the second button, too. And then the third, and pulled the shirttails out of the waistband of his slacks.

He caught Annie staring at him, an unreadable expression on her face. Mouth open, brows drawn, she clearly wasn't regarding him with anticipation. Or any of the eagerness his own body couldn't seem to control.

Perhaps she'd expected him to leave his shirt on.

Dropping his hands, Blake turned toward her, facing her across the room, with no idea what to say.

"I'm sorry, Annie," he finally rasped. "I have no idea how to give you a baby without making love to you."

"I know," she answered, as if she was fully prepared for the anticipated activity. Prepared, but not looking forward to it.

Frustrated, he began to wonder if he'd made a bigger mistake than he'd thought in coming here, agreeing to this.

And then he remembered why he'd said yes. The only reason. Because his friendship with Cole sure hadn't prompted his decision. He'd do a lot to honor that relationship, give the younger man the shirt off his back, even if it was the last one he had. But not this.

"Are you certain you want to go through with this?" he asked.

Her nod was tentative at best.

If not Blake, there would be someone else. Of that he had no doubt. He knew Annie too well. She might be vulnerable in places most people didn't see, but his lovely ex-wife was as determined as any human being could be. There was no stopping her, whether she was setting out, at age thirteen, to raise her eleven-year-old brother, as if they hadn't both just lost their father, and most of their mother's attention, too. At twenty, to put herself through college and work full-time. At thirty, to raise funds for battered women in San Antonio. Or at thirty-six, to have a baby.

And the idea of another man here, or in some clinic, impregnating the love of his life with a child who wasn't Blake's, had been more than he could bear the thought of. Since he'd had the choice. The idea of her being at risk to all the unknowns that could result from a stranger's participation in this event had been more than he could allow.

Since he'd had the choice.

"Help me out here." The words were almost torn from him.

She wrapped her arms across her chest. "I didn't think it would be this hard. This…awkward."

"How did you picture this happening?"

He and Annie had never talked about making love before. They'd just done it. Truth be known, they'd had a hard time *not* doing it. Anytime they were alone together. Sometimes it had seemed as if all it took was a look, a touch of their hands, and they'd be at it again.

"I didn't think about it." Her answer didn't make any of this any easier. "Not this part."

He'd liked to know what part she had thought about.

She waited, as if she was hoping he might figure it all out.

"I'd like to get undressed. If that's okay with you."

She nodded again. No more smoothly now than the time before. And her discomfort nearly broke his heart. He'd never, in all of his worst nightmares, imagined being alone with Annie and having her feel awkward. Unsure.

Of herself. Or him.

Even their first time—her first time ever—she'd been more eager and curious than apprehensive. He'd been the one trying to take things slowly. For her sake. Wanting to get her body ready, to introduce her to his in gentle increments, to ease the initial pain as much as possible.

All these years later, he could remember every detail of that time.

There was no chair for his shirt. Blake used the

door handle instead. Slid out of his shoes. And then his socks. His T-shirt followed. And he stood there again.

"Annie, I want to make this whatever you want it to be."

"Okay." Her response, her body, gave no indication what that might be. And Blake finally realized that she probably hadn't worked out any more of it than he had. Which changed things somehow.

"I don't know how to just have sex with you." Her indecision prompted his honesty. "I only know how to make love with you."

"Okay."

That stopped him. "Okay?" He held her gaze.

"Yes."

"You're sure?" She knew what he was asking.

They'd promised that they'd never, ever let their relationship get to the point where it was only sex between them. Never touch each other intimately if they couldn't do it lovingly.

"I'm sure."

Those two words were all the invitation Blake needed. He reached her in two strides, but he didn't immediately touch her. He couldn't yet. He'd been without her for far too long.

His heart ached with desire. And the knowledge that this wasn't real or lasting. A temporary pass to heaven.

For a moment, he wasn't sure he could continue, for fear of what would happen to him when they'd finished and he had to leave. Annie wanted him to touch her. He could feel her leaning toward him.

He just looked at her instead. At everything. The half-slumberous, half-uneasy expression in her eyes.

"They're as blue as I remembered them."

She smiled. But her lips trembled.

Taking in everything, her cheeks, her chin, he stopped at her throat. It was smooth and white and silky looking. Tenderness swelled and an unexpectedly sweet anticipation almost overcame him as he considered kissing her there again after all this time. And knew that he was going to be doing so. Very soon.

He trembled, faltered for an instant, as the full realization settled on him. This was happening.

After six long years, he was here in Annie's bedroom. About to touch her. To hold her again.

God couldn't have granted him a more precious moment.

Her breasts stood out against the silky gown, her nipples already hard. So, she wasn't as uninvolved as she'd looked. The knowledge calmed him. Gave him a confidence he hadn't known he'd lacked until that moment.

He might not understand the rules they were playing by, or even know the name of the game, but this was Annie. And loving her had always been natural to him.

"Come here," he said, waiting for her to step toward him before he touched her. This had to be what she wanted. Or it wouldn't happen.

It took her several long minutes, full of searching looks and silences. Just about the time Blake was convincing himself it wasn't going to happen after all, she took one step forward.

Where he got the willpower to wait for her to continue he had no idea.

When she took the second step, he almost moaned with the mixture of pleasure and pain that swept through him. Lifting his hand again, as he'd started to do earlier, he ran two fingers through her long curls. And then again. Pretty soon an entire hand was buried in the silky locks. And then both hands.

"Ah, Annie, you have no idea how good this feels," he said, shaking as he reacquainted himself with this first tender experience.

She didn't say anything, but when she shifted forward still more, pressing her mouth to his, Blake pulled her against him and thought that he wasn't going to ever let her go.

Even while he knew full well that, when he'd done what he came to do, he would, indeed, have to.

And never come back.

Annie might still share the intensity of his sexual desire, but beyond that there could be nothing between them.

She craved emotional strength and reassurance.

And Blake saw devils on his chest when he went to bed at night.

SHE'D PROMISED HERSELF to be detached, not to give in to the experience of being in Blake's arms again.

She'd promised herself not to lose all the strength and perspective and control she'd so painstakingly gained in the years since his disappearance. She'd promised herself that being with him one more time wouldn't matter.

And then he touched her.

Standing rigidly, Annie distracted herself with thoughts about nursery furniture, and yet she was completely, stunningly aware of Blake's fingers brushing her neck, her shoulder, as they ran through her hair. She analyzed the sensation—or tried to.

Her entire body weakened with the need for more. Thought was harder to hold on to. Focus impossible.

Instincts she didn't know she possessed took hold of her, wiping away memories that were too painful to bear, ideas and plans and thoughts that served no purpose here. She had to lean forward. To find his lips.

So she did.

And knew at once that she was in the right place. She belonged here. Blake's taste was exactly the same. As if she'd had her mouth open to his only moments before, instead of years. She hadn't even known he had a taste. Or that she'd recognize it again in an instant. His scent spoke to her, as well, as if it were a part of her. And she couldn't get enough of either.

She kissed him, again and again. Mindless of the fact that they didn't need to do this to make a baby.

There was strength here. Something much more

powerful than muscle or one person's determination. A cord that ran from some greater source through him to her. Pulling her in.

She had no chance to resist. No desire or power to resist.

And when his tongue met hers, she didn't remember why she could possibly have wanted to resist. Nothing was better than this. Nothing was safer or seemed more right than being skin to skin with Blake, connected to him, on the way to being one with him.

Unless it was the act itself.

NOT QUITE SURE HOW THEY'D gotten from half-dressed, beside the bed, to nearly naked and *on* the bed, Annie had at least one lucid moment when Blake reached for her panties.

She wanted them off as much as he did. Needed to make room for him. To invite him in where she needed him so badly.

To feel his hands upon her, working magic that only he could work.

To replace the feel of another man's hands, body, in a place she'd once promised Blake for all time and eternity.

And yet, as his fingers slid beneath the thin elastic band that ran across her hips, she hesitated, knew a moment of unease. Her frightened eyes sought reassurance from his. Or maybe understanding.

She could lose something vital in these next

moments. Exactly what, she couldn't grasp. She just knew that to allow this one last bit of lace to be eased away, to be so completely exposed to him, she was crossing a line and would never be able to come back. She'd no longer be free of him.

"You want to stop?" His voice was raspy, but his question completely sincere.

Did she? Trying to control her reasoning, Annie stared silently at Blake. Upon what should she base her decision? The past, which she couldn't remember at the moment? The future, which was unknown? Reason? A powerful need was running through her body, driving her onward to join with a force she'd existed without for far too long.

Blake drew back, gave her space, breathing room between them—time.

And then, with no articulate thought, no perception of making a decision, she slid her own fingers beneath the waistband of her panties, lifted her hips off the thin mattress and pulled them down, watching Blake's eyes follow every movement she made.

Loving the reverent, hungry look in his eyes.

"Yours, too," she whispered, locking her fingers on the elastic around his hips and easing his briefs downward.

He lifted up, but his arms buckled and then he caught himself. Attempted to help her, and got the waistband caught around his knee. Blake had never once shown a moment of awkwardness when they'd done this in the past, just a powerful drive to be one with her.

In his controlled, rather quiet way.

She'd loved that man. Loved everything about him.

She liked this one, too. Maybe even, in some small way, a little bit better. There was something about knowing that she could move him to the extent that he wasn't quite himself. That their time together mattered.

And then his underwear was on the floor with hers and he was back, sliding himself against her body, the hair on his legs brushing the skin of her thighs, and Annie wanted to laugh with sheer joy. To shout out the rightness of his return.

His fingers explored her feet and her calves, as he lightly massaged his way up her body. She lay there before him, completely comfortable now, secure in the knowledge that all their choices had been made and she was Blake's. For now. She would give herself up to needs and wants and desires that were far beyond her comprehension, her control. For a few short hours she would leave worries behind and just live.

And when, some time later, one knee found its way between her thighs, and his other leg followed, settling him in the crook of her body; when she opened to him completely, felt him nudging against her, searching, and finally, finally, sliding into her wet readiness, Annie started to cry with the wonder of it all.

After six long years, Blake truly had come home.

CHAPTER EIGHT

THERE WERE NO LIGHTS ON at the Wild Card Saloon when Blake pulled into the parking lot at five after seven on Wednesday night. The guys weren't due until 7:30, but Verne should be there, getting the cards out.

Getting a little drunk.

But then, Blake was forty-five minutes early. Time he'd allowed himself in case he'd had a call from Annie. In case she'd wanted to see him. She knew Wednesday nights were poker nights.

Was it only seven days since she'd crashed the party and made her absurd request?

And here he was, one short week later, possibly having fathered a child. Probably having fathered a child with her.

They'd not stopped at one try the night before, but had come together again and again, until Blake had been afraid he could stay awake no longer. And then he'd left, unwilling to risk a possible nightmarish episode.

One of the things he'd learned in his attempts to manage his condition was that any change in his environment or emotional status was likely to elicit an attack.

He made certain he was alone to handle them.

Thirty-five minutes until poker time and there were still no lights on in the saloon. There never were out front—not since Verne had let the place fall into such disrepair that, after only two years of managing it, he'd had to close the business. But there should be a light on in his apartment at the back.

Blake thought about waiting in his car. He didn't know Verne all that well, as the old man hadn't been part of the game six years before, when Blake had played with Cole and a few other guys in town. And in the two years he'd been back, Verne had only joined in the game a handful of times. Mostly he just came to collect the few bucks they paid him to let them use his place.

Whiskey money.

Blake didn't know Jake Chandler, Verne's nephew and the bar's true owner, at all, in spite of the fact that the younger man was an original member of the Wild Bunch. A throw-over title from the old days, when Cole and Jake and Brady and Luke had been at River Bluff High School together and had sneaked illegal games of Texas Hold'em in between all the other exploits they'd managed to dream up.

Blake would have liked to have known them back then. Hell, he'd have liked to have been a part of any group of friends. Growing up as he had—

on his own much of the time, while his uncle traveled, and then on the road himself, first with his uncle and then in his stead—Blake hadn't noticed the loneliness. It wasn't really until his return from Jordan, finding healing in the camaraderie of the old friends who'd accepted him as one of them as soon as Cole had pulled him back in, that he'd begun to realize all he'd missed.

No wonder Annie had struggled so hard to understand him. To believe he cared about her. She'd been seeking an emotional closeness that he hadn't begun to understand. Even if he had, on some level, recognized it, he'd certainly not have known how to express it.

Funny how having your freedom, your dignity, your very life stolen from you had a way of waking a man up to the deeper things in life. Of opening him up to his own needs. His own weaknesses.

Blake had been stripped of the defenses that had kept him safe, leaving him vulnerable and aware.

And still living alone.

As was Verne Chandler.

Half an hour to go, and there was still no sign of life in the old saloon. On his way to the back door, Blake dialed Cole's number. Left a message when the line switched over to voice mail. Cole had been Jake's best friend, back in the days of the original Wild Bunch, and had known Verne forever. His friend would be there soon.

In the meantime, Blake was going to try to make certain that the old man was just asleep—or someplace else, forgetting the time. Not that Blake held out much hope for the latter.

The elder Chandler was too eager for his money to miss unlocking the Wild Card's doors on Wednesday nights.

"Verne?" He knocked on the door leading into the back. "Verne!" he called again, after several knocks brought no response.

Looking for any sign of life on the upper level of the rickety old saloon, Blake made his way around to the front of the place, hoping to find Verne passed out on the broken-down veranda that, in its day, so he'd been told, had been one of River Bluff's most popular hangouts.

Verne wasn't there. Nor did he answer any of the other doors leading into the saloon.

Cole would be along any minute. As would Luke and Brady. And whoever else Brady, who was this week's host, had asked to fill the seats at the table that evening. Blake could wait for them.

Or he could go check the riverbank. Just in case.

He made his way down to the water in the dark. He'd taken the trip several times when he'd first started playing these weekly games. Back then, more than an hour in an enclosed place had had him jumping out of his skin.

None of the guys had ever said anything about his frequent absences, and as time went by, the need for them disappeared.

"Verne?" There was no sign of the old man along the edge of the river. "Verne!" No sign that anyone had fallen in, either, no broken brush. Or even freshly trampled weeds. But how would the man have managed to make it down here in a wheelchair? "Verne?"

Blake turned. Surveyed the area as best he could without a flashlight.

He'd once seen Cole grab a key to the back door from a crack in the old wooden windowsill by the kitchen. He could get inside.

At the least, maybe he'd find a flashlight stashed someplace.

Jake Chandler, a man who, from what Blake had heard from his friends, had been a rebel more because it had been expected of the bastard son of a town barkeep than because he'd been a bad kid, hadn't been home since he disappeared at eighteen. Hadn't been heard from since that time. Blake wondered what the man would think if he could see the place now.

Wondered what would happen to the Wild Card Saloon when something eventually happened to Verne Chandler, considering that his nephew, the actual proprietor, was nowhere to be found.

The key was right where he'd seen Cole find it. Feeling a little odd, Blake entered the darkened bar, turning on what lights he knew worked as he made his way farther inside.

"Verne?"

The card room looked as if no one had been in it since the game had ended the week before. There was still a bag of chips on a side table. And empty cans in the trash bin.

"Verne! You in there?" he called at the door to the apartment.

Flipping on a light, he made his way slowly, not wanting to startle the old man if alcohol had just made him hard of hearing.

The place was filthy. So much so that Blake raised a sleeve to cover his nose and mouth as the stench hit him. He found the source of at least one putrid smell all over the kitchen counter. Sour milk. And a tipped-over carton beside it.

"Verne?"

Still no answer. But yesterday's newspaper was open on the table.

"Verne!" He could see the entire apartment with a glance down the one long room. The only place left to check was the bathroom.

Moving quickly to the bathroom door, and growing more concerned by the second, Blake rapped.

What person who lived alone ever closed the bathroom door? Especially when one used a wheelchair most of the time?

"Verne?" After the second knock, Blake gave up all pretense of giving a damn about any possible invasion of privacy.

Shoving open the unlocked door, he stepped forward, to find the unconscious man lying prone on the floor beside the toilet, his pants down around his ankles.

ANNIE WAS ALMOST ASLEEP when Cole called just after the nightly news on Wednesday.

"What's wrong?" she asked, sitting up, instantly awake when she recognized her little brother's voice.

"Verne Chandler had a stroke." Cole's voice sounded strange. Lost.

"Is he alive?"

"For now. But he's still unconscious. Blake found him."

"When?"

"Tonight. He got to the game first and was concerned when he didn't see any lights on. If he hadn't found him when he did, and hadn't administered artificial respiration, Chandler probably would have died. Apparently, from what the paramedics and police could piece together at the scene, he'd been drifting in and out of consciousness since sometime last night. He must have just gone into cardiac arrest when Blake arrived."

It didn't surprise Annie a bit that her ex-husband had been the one to save the day. Or that he'd had the emotional wherewithal to remain calm and preserve a life.

"Has anyone called Mercedes?" she asked.

River Bluff's favorite postal worker had been married to and divorced from Verne before Annie could even remember knowing them. But she still kept an eye out for her ex, and Annie had always suspected that while the older woman hadn't been able, or maybe willing, to live with Verne's drinking, she'd never been able to fall completely out of love with him, either.

Verne Chandler, who'd come back to town upon his younger sister's death to assume responsibility for her saloon, and her then-twelve-year-old son, wasn't a bad person. He was just weak.

As Annie's father had been.

"She's with him now," Cole was saying, and Annie realized she'd missed the first part of her brother's response to her question.

"Thank God Blake was there," she said, wondering how Cole was taking this indication of another man being too weak to help himself, putting his life in danger rather than getting help. Especially when the man had been the father figure, however inadequate, of Cole's best friend during their pivotal high-school years.

"He was a rock," Cole agreed. Annie, still predisposed to mother her younger brother, hated the fatigue she recognized in his voice.

"Brady and Luke showed up before I did, and they were already cleaning up the mess before I even knew what was going on. When the rest of the guys showed up, I sent them home and then stayed to help get the place sorted out. It was a wreck."

Annie leaned over, elbows on her knees. She studied the hems of the sweatpants she'd thrown on after she'd realized that she couldn't possibly climb into the bed she'd shared with Blake the night before.

Not until she'd had time to put a little more

distance between that particular night and the rest of her life.

"Would you like to come over?" she asked. "There's still half a six-pack in the fridge." They'd shared more late-night beers than she could count in the months immediately following the breakup of Cole's marriage to a spoiled socialite who'd run home to Daddy after Cole lost his shirt in a real-estate deal she'd helped to orchestrate.

"No. I'm okay," Cole said, though he didn't really sound as if he meant it. "Blake stopped by and we had a couple of beers already."

Blake was still in town, then? Her stomach muscles fluttered, refusing to settle as she bade them to. They'd been acting up all evening, in spite of the fact that she'd made it perfectly clear to herself that Blake's presence in River Bluff for his weekly poker game had nothing to do with her. He'd been coming to town every week for the past two years, and she'd never once so much as seen him on the road.

Last night hadn't changed anything. He wasn't coming to see her.

To pretend that they needed one more night of loving in order to be certain she'd conceive the first time out.

"He said he was in town last night," Cole added, almost as an afterthought.

Except that she knew her brother.

"Oh." She wasn't discussing this with him.

"Said he was at your place."

"Yeah." Her tone dared him to make something of the fact.

"I'm glad. That's all."

"You pretty much ordained it," she reminded him.

"So, is everything…okay?"

"Fine," she said, aching to know what Blake had had to say about the night.

Aching to know, as always, the secrets so closely held inside Blake Smith's heart.

And the fact that she didn't know, had never known and *would* never know, was the reason why it was a damn good thing he hadn't stopped at her place before leaving River Bluff.

She couldn't fall for him again. Couldn't handle the doubts and insecurities, the jealousies that came with loving a man so private he couldn't even tell her he loved her. And every time she'd tried to coax his feelings out of him in words, every time she'd failed, she'd felt herself turning back into the frightened and confused thirteen-year-old who'd come home from school early with cramps to find her father in a body bag, and her mother being treated by the paramedics who'd answered her frantic call.

Annie had felt abandoned.

"We aren't getting back together, if that's what you're waiting to hear," she told her brother plainly, when it became clear that he was waiting for more.

"I didn't think you were."

"You hoped it, though. I know you, Cole."

"And I know you." Her brother's words were full of regret. "You're so locked into your idea of everyone else's expectations of what a healthy person looks like, and your own perception of a healthy relationship, that you can't see what's really there."

Sucking in her breath, Annie fell back against the beanbag chair, tempted to just hang up on Cole. "That has to be the cruelest thing you've ever said to me." She barely got the words out. Cole had always been her champion.

Her believer.

"It's not meant to be cruel, Anster," he said, the love in his voice doing something to soothe the wound he'd just inflicted. "It's meant to be an attempt to help. I'm scared to death that you're never going to be happy, because you're stuck in the mind-set of a frightened young girl."

Cole's words, on top of her own thoughts, hit Annie hard. Too hard for her to cope with so soon after the emotional experience she'd lived through the night before.

"Do you ever think about Daddy?"

"Sometimes. Mostly the good stuff. Especially now that I'm a carpenter again. Do you remember when he'd come in from the workshop, smelling like sawdust? And remember him taking us to Six Flags?"

At least half a dozen times.

"Yes." She'd been afraid of a costumed character once and her father had held her hand, walked her up to it and asked it to show her it was really a person with a big hat. The young man had quickly complied—though he'd taken them behind a building first. Annie's father hadn't laughed at her or told her it was ridiculous to be afraid. Instead, he'd treated her concerns with tenderness, respect and love. But she couldn't think about the good times much. They made what came after hurt that much more.

"Do you ever think about what he did?" she asked Cole. "Or wonder why?"

"Not if I can help it," Cole said slowly, his tone unusually serious. "I don't get it, Annie. And it's not like he's here to ask."

"I worry sometimes that I could be like him." She couldn't believe she'd put the words out there. Cole was quiet for so long, she wondered if he'd hung up.

"Me, too." His voice, when it came, was barely audible. "But I learned a long time ago not to dwell on what I had no control over and couldn't change," he added more strongly. "And that's where I worry about you. You've spent your whole life letting the event control you."

"I've grown up a lot in the past six years," she said, to remind her brother. And herself.

"I know, and I'm proud of you. I just want you happy."

"I am happy," she replied. And it was true, she had perfect moments. She just needed to have them a little more often. "Once I know there's a baby on the way, I'm going to be happier than I've ever been in my life."

"I hope so." Cole didn't sound at all sure of that. "I hope you aren't just bringing more hard times and loneliness upon yourself. Raising a baby alone can't be easy."

But Annie was no quitter. No weakling.

She was fully in touch with herself and what she had to have to experience life fully and completely.

ON THURSDAY, after discussing a series of prospective investments with Colin, who was in the office every day, Blake left work right on time to make it to the county hospital closest to River Bluff before visiting hours were over. There was no strong reason for him to be there, he acknowledged as he rode the elevator down from Verne Chandler's room. He'd heard from Cole, before he made the drive, that the old man was still unconscious. And that he was in the advanced stages of cirrhosis of the liver. But Blake had come anyway. River Bluff was calling out to him.

And while he wasn't fool enough to pretend that his recent encounter with Annie didn't have something to do with that, he was driven by more than just this impossible need to be close to his ex-wife. The acceptance he'd received from the Wild Bunch had been a far better cure for him than all the medications he'd been offered by his doctors.

And there was still one member of the Wild Bunch—in some ways the pivotal member—who didn't even know Blake Smith existed.

He couldn't do anything about that. Couldn't get to know a man who'd disappeared into thin air.

Yet, after last night, after breathing life back into

the man who'd helped raise Jake Chandler, he'd felt an odd kind of connection with the rebel who'd ridden out of town, never to be heard from again.

Verne hadn't moved at all during the half hour Blake had sat there with him. Likely hadn't known anyone was in the room. Blake was glad he'd come, all the same. Something had been served by the visit.

"Blake!" A surprised voice greeted him as the elevator door slid open on the first floor of the small county hospital.

"Luke, good to see you."

He shook the younger man's hand, appreciating the firmness of Luke Chisum's grasp. He identified with the young fighter, as he'd done since their first introduction the month before.

"How is he?" Luke asked, nodding toward the elevator, his cowboy hat in one hand, resting against a denim-covered leg.

"No change."

"He hasn't regained consciousness?"

Blake loosened his tie. "Not even for a minute."

"Not much reason for me to go up then, huh?"

"Probably not. They say he's not aware of anything at the moment."

Falling into step beside Blake as he headed back out to the parking lot, Luke said, "Wonder how they can tell that."

"Brain waves, I imagine."

He turned to say good-night as the cool October air hit him outside the hospital's revolving door.

And stopped when he noticed an unusual show of emotion on the cowboy's face.

"You got a minute?" Luke asked.

"Sure. What's up?"

"Want a beer?"

Blake hadn't had dinner yet. But a beer would suffice. He followed Luke across the street to a bar he'd visited more times than he liked to remember, when he'd first come home and had had to be near Annie, even though she'd thrown him over.

She'd been all there was to connect him to reality, to life after his long captivity, to hope and positive feelings. And the booze had helped him escape the rest of what he knew.

"I just got word this afternoon that a buddy of mine, my copilot, actually, was killed this morning in a raid outside Baghdad. He wasn't even on duty. Was in town trying to get a box of chocolates shipped to his mother, of all things."

Blake took a long swig of beer, blocking out the vision he had of the Middle Eastern desert and the towns that sprang up within it.

"There's no way to understand the harshness of life over there if you haven't seen it for yourself," Blake said.

"The people, so many of them, they live each day like they're running on batteries," Luke added. "You notice it right off when you first get there, and then, pretty soon, you look at yourself and you're doing the same thing, and you don't even know how you got that way." Luke nodded. "That's what happens after a while. It's a way of life and becomes commonplace, and you get so tired of being afraid that you just start accepting it all."

"Until you get home and the people around here have no idea about what any of that is like. And you want to be like them, but you aren't."

"You, too, huh?" Luke's grin was crooked.

"It gets better." Blake told him what he could. "The whole thing works in reverse, too," he continued, thinking of the parts of his life that had settled into a relatively comfortable routine. "After a while, surrounded by people who are more or less unaware of the darkest side of life on a daily basis, you start to adopt that as the norm."

CHAPTER NINE

THE ROADSIDE PLACE WAS quickly filling up, the evening's merrymakers occupying many of the tables and booths. And the more people that filtered in, the more Blake watched the door, keeping a line clear between him and it.

"I guess this whole thing just hit me harder today," Luke said, motioning for a second beer as their waitress hurried past, carrying a full tray. She took a second to smile at Luke, in a way that couldn't be mistaken.

"What with what happened with Verne and all," he continued, as if the woman hadn't been there at all. "I keep thinking about Jake, too, and how he took off out of here and none of us has ever heard from him again. I get him not contacting his uncle. It wasn't as if Verne was any kind of a father or guardian to him. And he certainly never came to Jake's defense when the town hung him out to dry for things he didn't do. But why wouldn't he contact one of us?"

Blake had some ideas about that. He just wasn't sure how to share them. Hadn't spent a lot of time sitting around trading confidences with a friend. Other than the beers he'd shared with Cole—who'd been his brother-in-law before he'd been his friend—he'd spent zero minutes in such a manner.

"We all have perceptions of ourselves," he said, choosing his words with care. "They aren't necessarily the way that others see us—though of course, we believe they are."

Luke was watching him, appeared to be listening. So Blake took a breath and continued.

"So maybe the guy Jake saw himself as isn't the same guy you knew him to be. Maybe he figured he really was the loser everyone in town had spent so much time telling him he was. He probably figured you were better off without him."

Just then, Wade Barstow, the man who owned half of River Bluff, came in. Took a seat at the bar. Even the lucky ones drank alone—and outside of town—sometimes.

"It's also possible," Blake continued, watching the successful rancher and taking comfort from his aloneness, "that Jake figures the rest of you did exactly what he did and got the hell out of Dodge, never to return." Forgetting the town patriarch, and his own wayward thoughts, Blake took a long sip of his beer.

"He wouldn't be too far off on that one," Luke said, staring down into his mug. "Cole's the only one who stayed in the area after graduation. But we all came back for visits. We all kept in touch."

"You had families to stay with when you came back."

And family made all the difference. Blake had learned that the hard way.

"So how do you do it, man?" Luke held Blake's gaze. "I saw some bad shit over there, but at least I was free to come and go. To decide what I wanted to eat. To choose my entertainment and sleep in a real bed. Being shot down was nothing, compared to what you went through. And you're a rock."

A rock. Talk about misperceptions.

"You just ride with it, take things in stride," Chisum continued. "Nothing gets to you."

Blake's first inclination was to ask the cowboy who'd paid him to say such things.

"There's got to be some trick to it," Luke continued, when he remained silent. "Some head thing you do."

"I just get up each day and keep breathing." Blake told Luke the part of the truth he could share.

"Do you ever think about not doing that?"

"Nope." Finally—an easy answer. "Never."

"Bec? It's me."

Back in the beanbag early on Thursday evening, Annie held the phone to her ear.

"Took you two days to call," Becky replied softly. "I was getting worried."

"I…" She didn't have an explanation.

"So how'd it go?"

"Good." Great. Sort of. The sex part was fabulous. The evening had been fabulous. Right up to the part where Blake pulled away from her, got up, put on his clothes and left, as if they hadn't just spent four hours joining their bodies time and time again, bringing each other a pleasure that was unsurpassable.

"And?"

"And now I wait a couple of weeks and do a home pregnancy test."

"That's it?"

Becky echoed the question that had been lodged in Annie's heart for two days.

"What else could there be?"

"You just slept with the love of your life, Ann. There could be all kinds of things. Not the least of which is regret."

"There's none of that."

"None."

"Okay." Already in the sweats she was planning to sleep in, she lay back against the pillow she'd brought in from her bed and pulled an afghan over her bare feet. "There's a little bit of regret."

"Tell me about it."

She wasn't sure she could. "I don't know. I'm not sorry for choosing Blake. Not sorry I might be pregnant."

"What, then?"

"I just…maybe…it was difficult, you know?" She finally said the words she'd spent forty-eight hours trying to avoid. And this was why she hadn't called her friend. Becky always knew. Always identified the things that Annie would prefer to hide away.

They were always the issues that, if left to fester, would get in the way of her happiness.

"Hard in what way?"

"To have him so close again, and then gone. I feel as if I've just lost him all over again."

Tears filled her eyes as she gave voice to the emotions she'd been trying to ignore. As though, if she didn't acknowledge them, pretended not to feel them, they couldn't hurt her.

"Ah, sweetie, this was exactly what I was afraid of."

"And you were right, Bec. I should have seen this coming. I'm an idiot."

"No. You're a woman who loved deeply and possibly forever. I think that on one level, you did see it coming, but there was this other part of you, obviously a bigger part, that needed to make love with Blake again. And that's why you did it."

Annie thought so, too. She just didn't know what to do about that.

"I can't get back with him."

"Has he asked you to?"

"No, and he's not going to."

"You could ask *him*."

"I can't, Bec. You know that. Blake's reserve hurt me so much it made me crazy—and then jealous. I can't live like that. I can't do that to him. And even if I could, I can't spend my life with someone who won't tell me he loves me. I spent too many years feeling abandoned and rejected."

"Your father's suicide had nothing to do with you, you know."

"Of course I *know* that, but it's as if I never quite *believe* it. If only I'd been more…something… Maybe it would have been enough to keep him alive, given him a reason for living."

"You just have to keep telling yourself that isn't true until you finally start believing it. You've been to all the classes and counseling sessions and read all the books, Annie. You know that suicide is the result of a person being in a place where the pain is worse than the coping skills. Period. It has nothing to do with anyone else."

"Unless something about me contributed to his pain and the loss of his coping skills."

"And what would that have been, sweetie? You were thirteen. And he was a manic depressive who went off his medication."

Annie had a tendency to forget that part sometimes. "I've never understood why he did that," she said now.

"Have you asked your mother?"

"Of course not. She practically had a nervous breakdown after Dad died. I've never dared broach the subject with her."

"It was a long time ago, Annie." Becky's soft voice was warm, and filled with compassion. "She's had a lot of time to recover. I bet she could handle that question now."

Annie rejected the idea immediately. But then she thought over Becky's words. It *had* been a long time. And she'd just considered the notion last week about how her mother might have made some changes that Annie had somehow overlooked.

Still…

"Maybe someday I will," she allowed. But not this week. Or next. Right now she had too many other things to deal with. She wasn't sure she had the capacity to handle whatever answers her mother might give her.

"How's your dad?" Blake asked Luke a couple of hours later as the two men walked back across the street to the hospital parking lot, where they'd left their cars.

Luke's father, Henry Oliver Chisum, founder of the Circle C Ranch, had suffered a stroke six months before, and the tall, proud cowboy now struggled to walk, even with a cane.

"He's good." Luke's voice might have had a bit of forced cheer to it. Blake couldn't be sure. "I tried to get him up on a horse yesterday, to bolster his spirits. They say that mind over matter can heal, but my dad wasn't having any of it."

"And your brother?" Had they not had a beer or two, Blake would probably never have thought to ask such a personal question. Wasn't even sure why he had, except that he'd heard the other guys ask that same question every single week since Luke's return.

He just wasn't sure why.

"Cantankerous as always." Luke's grin fell a

little short. "He's always resented me, though I've never quite been able to figure out why. This time around, I know why, though. He thinks I'm pushing Dad too hard."

"And maybe he thinks you're going to run out on him again." Blake had heard enough talk around the poker table to wonder if that was true, though only Luke would know. But by all accounts, Hank Chisum was a fair man. A likable one. A kind one. Except when it came to his much younger adopted sibling.

According to the other members of the Wild Bunch, Hank's attitude never made sense.

"Maybe he's afraid you're going to come in, stir things up and then be gone, leaving him to deal with the backlash."

"Maybe. Couldn't really blame him, I guess, but I'm not going to. I'm home to stay."

"I don't doubt you," Blake was quick to add. "Just trying to see things from Hank's point of view. The one left at home so often feels abandoned."

"Well, if that's what he's struggling with, he can get in line." Luke's sardonic reply was a step back from his usual jovial personality. Forced or not.

"I heard the guys razzing you about some girl you left behind," Blake continued. "She wanting to get in line, too?"

The grin he'd expected to see didn't appear on the cowboy's face. Nor was there even a hint of humor in his eyes.

"You could say that," Luke said, with more emotion in his tone than Blake had ever heard. "Becky's the nurse at River Bluff High School now, but when I knew her she was the most beautiful eighteen-year-old girl ever to have lived."

"You had it bad, huh?" Blake leaned an elbow against the Lincoln, commiserating with the other man.

"Worse than bad."

"So what happened? I'm assuming if she's sore at you for running out, she must have returned your sentiment. At least somewhat."

"Stupidity happened," Luke said, as if there was still some leftover bitterness from that particular sting. "Becky was the sheriff's daughter, and he'd made it known to all the boys that it was jail or hell if anyone messed with his daughter. So we all stayed clear of Becky. One night the poker guys and I were playing and getting a little drunk. They dared me to ask Becky for a date and I didn't want them to think I was chicken so I did. Becky and I hit it off and we became a couple around school. Then someone told her about the dare. I had forgotten about the stupid dare, but she was crushed, thinking I was talking to my friends about her. She wouldn't listen to anything I had to say. The sheriff told me he'd kill me if he ever saw me around his daughter again."

"And you believed him."

"I was eighteen." Luke pulled a set of keys out of the front pocket of his jeans. "My brother had been making life a living hell then, too. Jake had already skipped town. Brady was leaving. Cole was going to college. It was clear I wasn't going to be welcome running the Circle C anytime soon. Right about that time this army recruiter came through, promising us the world if we signed up."

"So you did."

"Yep." Luke tossed his keys in the air. Caught them. And headed over to his truck without another word.

NINE O'CLOCK. Annie had been talking to Becky for more than an hour, and still wasn't eager to hang up. To be alone with her thoughts. Much of the time they'd discussed a kid Becky had seen too many times at school. She suspected the young woman was being sexually abused by a family member.

Not the kind of thing they normally heard about in a small town like River Bluff.

Becky had been struggling incessantly, trying to figure out what she could and should do. And after weighing all the issues, she'd just decided to turn the case over to the authorities. If she was wrong, she could lose her job. If she wasn't, however, she might be saving a life.

"How's Shane been this week?" Annie asked as her friend seemed to come to peace with the decision.

"Okay." Becky drew out the word, making it sound as though she wasn't entirely sure. "He's doing his chores. Being respectful. He's in by curfew. And seems to be getting his homework done."

"But?"

"I think he's lying to me, Annie."

"About what?"

"That's just it. I don't know. It's just this feeling I get. But how can I call him on something that has no factual basis?"

"Just ask him if there's anything he's not telling you."

"I did."

"He denied it, of course. But what teenage boy wouldn't? Let's face it, he's fifteen years old. There are going to be things he isn't going to tell his mother."

"Like about the magazines under his bed?"

"Yeah."

"Did you ever tell him you found them?"

"No."

"Are they still there?"

"I have no idea."

"So what do you *think* the lies are about?"

There was a long pause. Staring at the shadows cast by the low lighting in the mostly empty room, Annie waited. And then asked, "Do you think it has to do with Katie?"

"Probably."

"I haven't seen any sign of him around here."

"He got caught there once. He's smart enough not to let it happen a second time."

"And he still denies having any association with her?"

"Completely."

"You're at school several times a week. Is there any way you can do some checking around?"

"Not without violating his trust. And I don't think I'm ready to do that yet."

The pain and confusion in Becky's voice jolted Annie's heart.

"If you had it to do over again, Bec, would you still have had Shane?"

"Absolutely."

"Even being a single parent?"

"It wouldn't have been my first choice by a long shot. It's a lot harder raising a child without someone there to back you up. But yes. I absolutely would do it all over again."

They'd had the discussion before. Many times. A lot recently, as Annie had started entertaining the idea of having a family of her own. But things looked different when you were in the middle of them. And those were the times Annie most needed to be prepared for.

And she'd been thinking about them a lot in the last forty-eight hours.

"Do you ever think about what kind of father Luke might have been, if things had worked out differently and you'd married him instead of Danny?"

"Not anymore." Becky's reply was too quick and too loud.

"Really?" Annie pushed, just as Becky would have done with her. It was what they were about—helping each other to be honest with themselves. To face life head-on instead of running from it. "Not at all?"

"I don't think so," Becky said. "Of course I'm thinking about him. How could I not be? River Bluff's a small town. I can't even go downtown without the risk of seeing him."

"Maybe if you talked to him it would help."

"How? What could I possibly say—what could he say, for that matter—that would change anything?"

"I don't know. He might tell you that it broke his heart to leave town sixteen years ago. Maybe explain why he went."

"It would be good to hear." Becky sounded as though she might start to cry. "But I can't chance it," she added. "Not with him planning to stay here. I can't put the past to rest at the risk of jeopardizing the present."

"And you think speaking to Luke would do that?"

"Yes." Her tone was unequivocal.

"Why?"

"Because once we open that door, where are we going to go from there?"

"Who knows?" Annie thought about Blake. About possibilities. And impossibilities. "Maybe you could be friends."

"No." Another definite response. "I loved him too much for that."

Annie's heart ached for her friend.

"Maybe, if you talked to him, you'd find out that things have changed. That you've changed. Maybe it was just a puppy love that has lingered in your mind, grown larger for the lack of resolution, and it would fade away if you gave it a chance."

"Is that what happened with you and Blake?"

The question stopped Annie short.

But at the same time, it was comforting to know she wasn't alone. That maybe Becky would understand the sudden doubts that were assailing her. Frightening her with their intensity. Their waywardness.

Was she not as healthy emotionally as she'd believed she was? Had she just convinced herself out of a need to make it so?

Pulling her legs up Indian style beneath her, Annie hugged the pillow to her midsection. "Can I tell you something?"

"Of course."

"Several times over the past day and a half I've hoped that I'm not pregnant."

The resulting pause scared her. "You've changed your mind?" The question came slowly, as though Becky didn't quite understand.

"No." Annie didn't think she had. Unless she wasn't going to be stable enough to be everything her child would need her to be.

"Then what?"

She was embarrassed to say. Afraid to say. Afraid to know what it all meant.

"If I'm not pregnant, then I'll have an excuse to make love with Blake again."

The words were worse said out loud than they'd been in her head.

"Don't you think that's telling you something?"

"He's a great lover." The statement was beneath her.

"It's just physical, then? There's nothing wrong with that between two consenting adults."

No, it wasn't just physical. The sensual aspect of her encounters with Blake, while phenomenal, had always been more like a wonderful bonus than the substance of what they shared. She'd always believed that was what had made them so great.

And was the source of her problem now.

"You knew I was still in love with him, didn't you?" A tear dripped onto her pillow.

"I was pretty sure."

"So why did you let me do this? Why didn't you tell me?"

"Would you have believed me?"

If anyone could have convinced her it would have been Becky. But… "Probably not." Annie had been so certain she was in complete control.

A hard-won control that had given her the confidence to think she could be a mother. And cope with anything.

"Maybe loving him isn't a bad thing." Becky's voice was soft, but not tentative. "Did you ever think of that?"

Both cheeks wet with tears, Annie shook her head. And then realized her friend couldn't hear that.

"It is a bad thing, Bec," she said, knowing that she spoke the truth. "Whatever pulls the two of us together also keeps us apart. We aren't good for each other on an elemental level. Our love hurts us, because we're both so aware that we're letting the other down. But it's in ways we can't help."

Those words didn't sound good out loud, either, but they rang true.

"That's one of the saddest things I've ever heard," Becky said.

"I know."

"We're a pair, aren't we?" Becky asked, and Annie thought she detected a hint of a smile in her friend's words—and tears there, too.

"I love you, Bec."

"I know. I love you, too."

CHAPTER TEN

ONE OF THE THINGS Blake had learned in his two years of struggling with the gift of getting his life back was that he would not ever, ever get behind the wheel of a moving vehicle after having more than two beers. He'd done it once. And missed hitting an innocent child by about two inches.

The incident had sobered him for good. He'd not been drunk since.

And he wasn't tonight. But he'd had three beers.

As soon as Luke was gone he relocked the Continental and, pocketing his keys and cell phone, set off on foot. He'd hitchhike into town. Maybe stop and get a sandwich someplace. As small as River Bluff was, he'd have to go twice around the town before he figured he'd be ready to head back to his car and return to San Antonio, unless he found somewhere to stop off first.

He headed down Main Street. Past the Longhorn Café. Sandra, the night waitress, was on duty tonight. He could see her in the window. Pretended not to notice her welcoming smile as she spotted him.

He'd been in one too many Wednesday nights in

a row. Must have given Sandra the wrong impression. Blake was definitely not interested in a night or anything else with her, and he walked on past.

No one was hanging around the *River's Run* building, like one might see outside the *San Antonio Gazette*. Or, he expected, any other major paper across the nation. Passing a couple of gift shops, a lawyer's office and a barbecue place, Blake headed toward the clinic and the houses beyond. He could always walk out to Cole's place. If his friend was there, he'd have something for Blake to eat, pour him some black coffee and then drive him back to his car.

And if Cole wasn't there, Blake could let himself in with the key his friend had given him, and wait for him.

He could also keep walking.

Or he could quit lying to himself—something he swore he'd never do intentionally to counteract those times his head played tricks on him and led him to believe things that didn't actually exist—and just admit that he knew where he was going.

The place he'd been longing to visit for the past forty-three hours and twenty-one minutes.

The place he'd known he'd end up at when he left his office in San Antonio earlier that evening.

He had no business being there. Couldn't stay. Was under no illusions whatsoever regarding the future. But he thought he could justify one more visit.

ANNIE WOULD HAVE LIKED to be falling asleep half an hour after hanging up the phone with Becky.

Instead, she was lying on her makeshift bed on the living-room floor, staring up at the ceiling and looking for honesty, if nothing else. Her cheeks sticky with the residue of tears, she thought about getting up and going to her real bed. Running from it was stupid. Immature.

She thought about taking a hot bath.

Or calling her little brother. ·

She thought about…

Answering the door? Who would be dropping by at 9:30 on a Thursday night without calling first?

Tugging down the wrinkled and worn Texas A & M T-shirt she'd pulled on over her sweats, Annie ran for the door, fearing bad news. If something had happened to Cole, or June or…

"Blake?"

She glanced past him, wondering if Cole was with him. And didn't see a car. "How'd you get here?"

"Walked. My car's still out at the hospital."

"Why?" She stood in the doorway, frowning, trying to make sense of what was going on. To figure out what was wrong.

"I left it there. Hitched into town, didn't think I should drive."

"Have you been drinking?" He didn't look like it. Or smell like it. But…

"I had a few beers with Luke earlier."

How many were a few? Blake had never been a heavy drinker.

"Not really enough to do damage, but I don't take chances."

That sounded familiar. "Is something wrong?"

"Maybe."

Realizing that she was keeping him outside, Annie stepped back and held open the door. "Would you like to come in?"

He moved past her, continuing into the living room. And stood staring at the pillows and blankets spread on the floor. A cord dragged across the middle of the room, leading to the alarm clock she'd set to the right of her makeshift bed.

"You have a guest."

"Just me."

His gaze was piercing. "This is for you?"

"Yes." She looked straight at him, daring him to make something of the information. Let him think she was crazy. Didn't matter to her one way or the other what Blake Smith thought of her.

Because no matter how she did or didn't feel about him, he was not going to be a part of her life.

Other than if you've conceived, in which case he'll be stopping by to pick up his child for visits occasionally, a little voice reminded her.

If she were pregnant now, she could end up seeing Blake on a regular basis for the rest of her life. The prospect was almost as painful as it should have been. How could she possibly think that seeing a man whom she loved but could never have on a regular basis was a good thing? Unless she was some kind of masochist.

Her father had been the ultimate masochist. He'd

hurt himself to the point of choosing to die. Raising a gun to his head and pulling the trigger.

Spilling blood all over the floor of his shop.

"What?" she said, as Blake continued to watch her.

"You used to do that," he stated.

She wrapped her arms around her middle, wishing she had a pillow to hold. "Do what?"

"Go off someplace. I never knew where you went, but you always got that same pained expression on your face."

No one had ever told her that. Not even Becky. Annie would have liked to know. Had no idea that her expression was so readable.

"Why didn't you ever ask me about it?"

Hands in his slacks pockets, he stood there, looking more handsome than any forty-year-old man had the right to look after a full day's work and a walk from the outskirts of town. "I figured if you wanted me to know, you'd tell me."

Such a Blakelike response. And so frustrating.

"I didn't know you even noticed," she said. "Or cared what I thought about."

"Of course I cared!"

"You never said you did."

"I wouldn't have married you, if I didn't care."

She stood toe to toe with him, chin slightly raised as she looked him in the eye. "Caring takes many forms, Blake. You have to communicate what you want for other people to understand and give it to you."

"I've never been much of a talker. You know that."

She did know. And here they were, after six years of separation, right where they'd been so many times before in their relationship. Caring, but unable to connect on that deep level that kept two people together.

Or at least gave them a hope of making it.

"Why'd you come here tonight?"

He glanced down. "Why are you sleeping on your living-room floor?"

Annie thought about telling him her bed frame had broken. Or that she had a leak in the bedroom ceiling. She was tempted. But she'd never been able to lie to Blake.

Knowing she was probably going to regret having him know the truth, she said, "Because I couldn't get back in my bed after sharing it with you."

She'd made it through the confession without showing obvious emotion. Inside, however, she was falling apart. She needed this man. God, how she needed him. Just for now. For tonight. Just for a moment. While she figured out where she went next in this crazy life of hers.

It happened every time. Just as soon as she thought she had things in order, as soon as she was on board with the plan, there was another twist.

"Why not?" His words were dangerously soft. He hadn't moved, but he felt closer.

"I was afraid I'd miss you too much."

His eyes narrowed. Darkened. "You want me back in your bed?"

Annie shrugged uncomfortably. Not liking the way he was putting her on the spot.

"Why did you come, Blake?"

"The same reason you're sleeping on your living-room floor."

Yeah. She'd been afraid of that. And hoping for it, too.

"What are we going to do?"

"Do you want me in your bed tonight, Annie?"

"You know the answer to that."

"I want to hear you say it."

"Why?"

"You're the one who says words are so important."

Tilting her head, Annie studied him. From the short tousled hair, past the tie loosened at his neck, the legs that seemed to go on forever. "What do *you* want, Blake?"

"My needs are simple," he said. "I want to lie in your bed, take you in my arms and forget that there are a million reasons I shouldn't be there."

She wanted that, too. Making love with Blake again wasn't going to solve anything. Or change anything.

Grasping his hand, she started to lead him back to her room.

He didn't budge.

"What?" she asked, glancing back at him. And only then realized how horrible she must look. Old sweats. Hair tangled around her shoulders and down her back. Tear-streaked, makeup-free cheeks.

She wasn't a twenty-year-old anymore, who could get away without the camouflage makeup provided.

"Say it, Annie. Tell me that you want me in your bed tonight."

Why she resisted, Annie wasn't sure. But something stopped her from doing what he asked.

"We aren't good for each other, Blake."

"I know that."

His easy acquiescence surprised her. And saddened her. Though she'd known the truth, his validation still hurt. Which only proved the danger she was in, standing here talking to him. Contemplating more.

"We're too different. Our personalities, emotional needs, they don't complement each other."

"I know, Annie."

Sincerity rang in his words. And, surprisingly, calmed her.

"And you still want to spend the night in my bed."

"I still want to take you into my arms and hold you awhile."

It made no sense, what they were doing. And yet it felt completely right.

"I want you in my bed tonight, Blake."

She knew, as soon as she said the words, that she'd just crossed another line, into territory so unfamiliar she'd have no hope of traveling there without getting lost.

BLAKE MOVED SLOWLY, entering Annie, pulling back, returning and finding peace, as well as passion in the movement. He'd loved her well that night, finding things in her he'd never found anywhere before in this life of his. Giving and caring, certainly, but so much more than that. She accepted him just as he was now, without any expectations. Or a need for things he'd never be able to give her.

In Annie's arms, he was finding unconditional love—something he'd lost in the crash that had taken his parents when he'd been too young to completely understand the changes that had been wrought in his life.

This was the third time they'd come together that night. Silently. Seemingly understanding that words would only come between them, not help them. He reached for her and she was there. She reached for him and he couldn't deny her.

He loved her slowly this time. Savoring every nuance, every sensation, his eyes focused completely on hers as he slid in and withdrew in long, slow strokes, no less passionate for their lack of fervor. He'd stripped her of her clothes hours before—and she'd reciprocated.

Her bare breasts, nipples erect, brushed against him as he moved, back and forth, and the friction through the hair on his chest was just one more sensation to take in. To appreciate.

There was no doubt in Blake's mind that he loved her. Had always loved her. Just as he knew he never wanted to hurt her by imprisoning her within his emotional voids. He didn't look for a happy ending here. Only a moment. A touch of heaven to take with him into the darkness.

He could feel the pressure burning within him, building—and he tried to hold on. He didn't want to spill into her, to end it. And at the same time, he had to give himself to her completely, to know that moment of total release.

"I want you to come with me." He hardly recognized his ragged whisper.

Then he helped her, waiting for her moans of pleasure, the deepening tone that told him she was close. And when she got there, when he felt her start to pulse around him, Blake slid into her one more time, held himself there and offered a silent prayer of thanks.

A BABY LAUGHED. Feeling strong, capable and knowing, Annie moved toward the sound, aware that she couldn't touch the child, couldn't speak to it or interact in any way. She was there simply to watch over. To protect and guide. Not to be known. There was a woman with the child: her friend Becky. Annie smiled, only a little sad as Becky scooped up the baby, hugging her to her breast, kissing her neck, inhaling her sweet scent. Becky was truly happy, and that was good. She loved her little girl. She was content and at peace and hopeful. She was looking forward to that evening, when she and her husband were celebrating their second anniversary. Annie sensed her feeling these things. She wanted to reach out to her old friend. To let her know she was there. That all would be well. To tell Becky that she had another fifty years with the man she adored. And that even when they died, they'd be together still.

But she couldn't. It was against the rules to interfere. She might lose her position if she tried to spoil the way life must unfold. And this job was too precious to her. Too vital. She was who she was meant to be. An angel. Watching over all. Never to be loved for herself. But always to love...

The movement startled her, jerking Annie from a warm, if slightly bittersweet place, making her forget, even as she remembered the strange dream. And then, fully awake, she remembered too much.

Blake. Lying in his arms as she fell into an exhausted sleep. Completely peaceful. Having loved with her whole heart.

He was leaving her. She watched him in the shadows as he collected his clothes from the floor, stepping into them quietly. She had no idea of the time; her clock was still out on the living-room floor. But she knew the night had to be at least half-over.

And Blake didn't have a car here.

"Let me drive you," she said softly, sitting up.

He jerked around, and she knew he'd wanted to go without waking her. Without facing her.

"I need the walk."

"Not at three in the morning," she said, having glanced at her watch as she switched on the light.

Blinking, Blake shook his head. "I'm not having

you get up and go out at this time of night," he told her. "I don't want you out driving alone."

He could follow her back. They both knew that. Just as she knew that Blake needed to get away from her now. She wanted to understand why. Tried not to be hurt by the knowledge.

And didn't really succeed at either.

"My keys are in the tray in the kitchen," she told him, lying back down and turning off the light. "I don't need the car until Saturday."

Blake hesitated, and she was afraid he was going to refuse even this little bit of her help. And then he nodded and she relaxed against the pillows.

"Thanks," he said. And without so much as another look back, let alone a kiss or a hug, or a promise to come again, he left the room.

Lying there alone, Annie listened for the sound of her keys being picked up, heard him open and close the door leading into the garage. Waited while he started her car and drove away.

And then she cried herself back to sleep.

JUNE STOPPED BY THE *River's Run* office on Friday morning to ask Annie if she had time for lunch. It was a regular occurrence between mother and daughter. June asking. Annie declining, and feeling as if she'd done them both a favor. She let June feel she was doing her part as a mother without holding her accountable for any motherly deeds.

"Please, Annie," June said that morning. "I'm worried about you. Can't you spare half an hour and split a sandwich at the Longhorn with me? Just long enough to talk for a bit?"

If Annie hadn't been so tired, she might have been better able to ward off the confusion that swamped her at the unexpected switch from their established routine.

"I'm fine, Mom, really," she said, trying to understand what the expression on her mother's face meant. It reminded her of something, and for a long time she couldn't place it.

But late that afternoon, long after June had left to have lunch by herself, it came to Annie. She knew why that look on her mother's face had been so familiar. It was the same expression she'd seen on her own face the night before. In the dream that had been interrupted by Blake's departure.

The look of an angel, glancing down with compassion and tenderness and the promise of infinite love for those in her care.

And that made absolutely no sense at all.

WHEN BLAKE CALLED ANNIE on Friday evening, asking if he could drive her to the hospital to exchange cars, she wasn't surprised. She'd been waiting to hear from him.

And when, after the exchange, he followed her home and into her house, she wasn't surprised, either.

She'd known he would. That he'd be back in her arms again that night. She offered him a glass of wine.

He declined.

An omelet.

He declined that, too.

"I haven't had dinner yet," she said. "You want to order a pizza or something?"

"You call, and I'll go pick it up," he replied, retrieving his keys from the counter where he'd dropped them.

He could provide his own dinner. And dinner for her. He couldn't accept something she made for him. She got that, too.

"We have to talk about the baby." Biting into a piece of pizza that she didn't want at all, Annie forced herself back to reality. To the life that she was going to have to start living again.

Blake stopped, a piece of pizza halfway to his mouth. "You already know you're pregnant?"

She couldn't tell if he was relieved, horrified, or if he even cared at all. "There are some over-the-counter tests that claim they can tell three days after conception, but no, I don't know I'm pregnant."

Annie couldn't help remembering the last time they'd done this—discussed a baby they'd made together. And how very different, and yet completely the same, it was. Blake hadn't shown much emotion then, either. Not even when she'd told him that she'd been to the doctor and knew for sure that they were finally going to have the baby they'd been trying for.

When he'd left on that business trip, she hadn't

even been certain that he wanted the child she was carrying.

"The results really aren't going to be accurate unless I wait a couple of weeks." She wasn't sure why she continued to speak to him about things he clearly had no interest in.

"So we'll talk then."

And that was that. Regardless of the million and one questions rattling around in Annie's brain.

Things such as, If I am, are you really going to insist on some kind of shared parenting arrangement? Am I going to have you skating around the perimeter of my life forever?

Tempting me to invite you into my bed forever?

Am I always going to hurt like this?

They were questions she couldn't ask. Not because he wouldn't answer them, although she suspected that he wouldn't, but because she couldn't have him know how out of control she really was.

And that night, after Blake loved her, and left without falling asleep in her arms as she'd invited him to, she knew she couldn't spend the rest of her life with the feelings of abandonment he always caused.

Their lovemaking interlude had been an incredibly precious three days. And now it was over. She would not be inviting Blake into her bed again.

CHAPTER ELEVEN

"MR. SMITH, you got a minute?"

Blake dropped the proposal he'd been reading, leaving behind the fine print with regret, as his new semi-employee approached him Monday afternoon. Blake had been fully engaged, focused, in the realm where he was confident and sure and had complete faith in himself.

"Sure, Colin." He waved the young man in, indicating a seat across from his desk. Still not completely sure why the young man was there, or why he'd allowed him to stay, Blake was somewhat curious as to what the college graduate would have to say.

"I found that horse."

He hadn't expected that. "You did." Impossible. Or nearly so. Folks spent years looking at breeders, bloodlines, wins. Assessing data and percentages, visiting farms, scrutinizing sires and mares, living conditions and owners, before they even considered spending the kind of money Blake had been talking about when he'd sent Colin on a search for a possible horse for Brady Carrick.

"It's the perfect horse," the young man said, the same passion in his voice now as he'd had when he'd sold himself to Blake. "It's in Dallas."

"You can't buy a horse sight unseen," Blake said, enamored enough with the boy's enthusiasm to be willing to have patience, to teach him a thing or two.

"I'm not suggesting that anyone do that."

"We can't recommend him to the Carricks, sight unseen." Blake made his point more clear.

"I wouldn't suggest that, either, sir."

"Then…"

"I drove up to Dallas over the weekend," Colin surprised him by saying. "It's a seven-month-old weanling that isn't even broke to bridle yet. He's the one. I'm telling you, sir, I know he's the one."

Blake didn't know any such thing. But hand on his chin, he sat back, assessing his new employee, wondering what quirk of fate had sent him to Blake, and whether or not he was going to be a gift or a curse.

"Go on," he said, in deference to the fact that he didn't yet know which Colin was.

"His sire is Macintosh Red from Dufoil Stables in Virginia. You've heard of him, haven't you?"

"Who hasn't?" Blake asked, repeating back to the boy the words he'd used when Blake had asked him if he'd ever heard of Brady Carrick and the Cross Fox Ranch. "He won the Arkansas Derby, the Arlington Million and the Oak Leaf Stakes."

Colin seemed neither impressed nor unimpressed by Blake's knowledge. "The dam is Honey's Gold from Henleys' Blue Bonnet Farm."

"This horse is at Henleys'?"

"The Carricks have known Al Henley for years," Colin told Blake.

Was this kid a private eye in his spare time? "And how do you know that?"

"The sale of horses is public record," Colin said. "The two farms have had several business dealings, dating back a number of years."

Good, solid information. Blake wasn't ready to be impressed, but at least Colin had his full interest. "Go on."

"He's chestnut colored with white socks. His neck is long and his hocks and knees are perfectly straight. His hips are maybe a little narrow, but it doesn't affect his stride at all."

"How do you know so much about horses?"

"I don't," Colin said. "But I know someone who does, and I took her to Dallas with me for the weekend."

Ah. A man with contacts. And the sense to use them.

"He's being offered at a private sale on January 16, and I'm betting the Carricks can get him for forty to forty-five thousand. He's a winner, Mr. Smith. You aren't going to find a better horse."

Eyes narrowed, Blake studied the kid. "You're sure about that."

"Absolutely."

There was nothing cocky in Colin's attitude.

Nothing unlikable at all. He was someone who knew what he was talking about, and was certain he was making the best recommendation.

Blake considered his options. To tell the kid to go back to the drawing board just in case. To continue researching because he hadn't been at it long enough. To go away and never come back. Or to give him a chance to sink or swim, to believe him and find out what the kid was really made of...

"I'll give the Carricks a call," he told the boy. And pretended not to notice when Colin gave a short, completely unprofessional whoop of joy.

"You won't be sorry, Mr. Smith," he said, slightly more collected as he shook Blake's hand and hurried out to his desk in a cubicle behind Marta's.

For better or worse, it looked like Blake had a new kid in the house.

ANNIE HAD WAITED for Blake Saturday night, having spent the day determining exactly what she was going to say when she sent him away. And again on Sunday. But he didn't show up either night. Didn't call.

By Monday evening, after two sleepless nights thinking about him, running scenarios and outcomes through her mind, plus spending the weekend trapped at home for fear he might show up and she'd miss him, she knew she couldn't go on like this. She had no desire to chase after Blake. Or to hound him. But she had something to say and a need to say it.

She dialed his cell phone on the way home from work, holding her own cell to her ear as she bicycled slowly through the streets of River Bluff—taking the long way because she needed to feel the wind in her hair.

"Annie?" He answered on the second ring. And obviously knew her number, since he seemed to have recognized it on his phone.

"Yes."

"Is something wrong?"

"No." Not exactly. He sounded so good. Alive and vital. Real. It was good to hear his voice. "Am I interrupting something?"

"I'm still at the office," he told her. "Just finishing up a proposal."

Had he been planning a drive to River Bluff after that? Annie quivered at the possibility of one more night in his arms. Considered asking him to come, just in case she'd been off a day or two on her fertility charts. As a safety measure.

"A proposal for something you're considering buying?" she asked. She'd never had a lot to do with Blake's work when they'd been married. The business had been between him and his uncle. Something they'd always shared. A bond between them. Asking about it had always felt to Annie as if she'd been intruding on their parenting of a beloved child.

"A condo conversion." His voice took on the confidence of the successful businessman he was as Blake gave her a brief overview of his newest project. It sounded impressive. Far-reaching. And a little bit risky.

"You really think people are going to buy apartments?" she asked him, thinking about the real-estate column she wrote for the first Monday edition each month.

"These projects have seen overwhelming success in L.A. and Phoenix."

"Mind if I pick your brain for a column in a couple of weeks?" Annie asked after he had given her more details.

"Of course not." His reply was more than just welcoming. He sounded genuinely pleased to help her. Honored even.

And that was her clue.

"I called to tell you that…"

Did she really want to do this? Cut herself off from something that gave her more…everything…than anything she'd ever known?

Did she really want to spend the rest of her life crying herself to sleep alone in the bed her lover had just left?

"What is it, Annie?"

"I…missed you over the weekend."

His silence unnerved her. Embarrassed her. She'd had expectations when there were to be none.

"And the fact that I did brought home to me quite clearly something I'd already determined."

"And what is that?"

"I… Just in case you were thinking about coming back…"

Another silence. He wasn't helping her out at all. Except that maybe he was. Blake's silences were a good part of the problem between them. He couldn't end them. She couldn't live with them.

"I can't do it, Blake." The words, when they came, did so in a rush. "I can't make love with you again."

"I understand."

"You do?"

"Yes, Annie, I do."

"And you're not mad?"

"Not at all. How could I be?"

Because she owed him nothing, he meant? Or because he cared too much about her to be angry, when she had to make a hard decision in order to take care of herself?

"Okay, then, well, I'll talk to you later..."

There was nothing more to do but hang up. Annie rode along, phone to her ear.

"Annie?"

"Yes?"

"You'll give me a call? Next week when you do the test?"

The test. The baby they might have made. That he wanted to father.

"Yes. Of course."

Annie was blinking tears from her eyes, furious with herself, with Blake, with a fate that would show her the magnitude of love, only to dangle it just out of reach, when she rounded the corner to her street minutes later and noticed someone stumbling about in her front yard.

Someone young. Male. With dark hair. In Wranglers, a T-shirt and sneakers. No sweater, in spite of the sixty degree weather. She knew him.

"Shane?" she asked, sliding to a quick halt and hopping off her bike. "What's wrong?"

The young man's skin was pasty looking. His eyes were big, his pupils distorted. He took a step and almost fell.

"I don't feel so good." His slurred words made her bristle, even as Annie's heart went out to Becky's son.

"You've been drinking, huh?" she asked, slipping an arm around his back, intending to get him inside—and sober—before his mother saw him. Becky would hear about this. Annie just didn't want her friend to see it.

Bec already had too much on her plate. Too much she ate herself up with guilt about.

"N-no, Annnnnie," he stuttered. "I ssswear."

He stumbled again, falling into her with a whoosh of breath against her face, and the first bit of alarm raced through her. She'd been around drunk people enough times to know that their breath reeked. And that they didn't usually stutter.

Maybe Shane wasn't drunk.

"What did you take?" she asked, brusque with worry and a need to get help in case his life was in danger.

"N-notth-thing," he said, his eyes wide and frightened as he leaned against her. And Annie believed him. His pupils were dilated. That couldn't be good.

"C-c-c-ould you c-call my mom?" His stutters were getting worse.

Annie had to get him inside. And call for help. Cell phone at her ear, she did both at once.

"BLAKE, GOOD TO SEE YOU." Dr. Elizabeth Magnum shook his hand, joining him at the conversation pit in her downtown San Antonio office Monday evening. "It's been awhile."

The doctor was in her late fifties, with short salt-and-pepper hair and broad shoulders, and Blake found her comforting to be around. As did hundreds of other people, if her extensive client base was anything to go by. She wore no jewelry. Not even a wedding ring. He had no idea if she was married, had family or lived alone as he did.

"Thanks for working me in." Pursing his lips, Blake sat in his usual chair, across from the doctor's corner of the couch. "I thought I was better."

"You are better. Amazingly so."

He loosened his tie. "My night stalker has returned."

"Are you taking your Desyrel?"

"For the last two nights. Fifty milligrams." The sleep aid's minimum dosage.

"And before that?"

Hands on the arms of the chair, Blake focused on relaxing his muscle groups, one at a time. "Not for about six months."

"With no problems sleeping?"

"They were minimal." He'd been experiencing

bouts of insomnia since he was a kid—probably since his parents' car accident, but he didn't know that for sure. Those he could deal with.

"How are you doing with the alcohol consumption?"

"No problems at all."

"And depression?"

"I'm good there." Never had had much of a problem in that area, if you disregarded those first couple of months he'd been back in Texas—and that had been completely understandable. He'd lost a child, a wife and an uncle in one fell swoop.

Dr. Magnum looked down at the folder in her lap, as though checking Blake's records—except that the blue file was still closed. "You know the three categories of symptoms," she said. "Tell me where you're at."

"Flashbacks had lessened, but I've had a few lately. One episode of completely reliving the event—felt as if I was there, was shocked to come out of it and find that I wasn't." Category one. "A guy in my poker game recently returned from Iraq. We met for drinks last week and he talked some. I'm not going to Wednesday night's game. Have twice picked up the phone to bow out of the game permanently. Haven't been able to read even so much as a headline about Iraq all week."

Category two.

"And aside from my nocturnal pal, an engine backfired on the way to work this morning and I almost ran my car into a ditch."

Category three.

And the seal on Blake's fate. With symptoms in all three categories, he still fit the official diagnosis of post-traumatic stress disorder.

A fate almost worse than death, as far as he was concerned, as it trapped a man in an emotional whirlwind that prevented him from living a normal life. Interfered with relationships. With family ties. With a man's very ability to love.

"Any outbursts of anger? Problems concentrating?"

"No." Not since those first couple of months.

"What about relationships? Other than the soldier, how are you getting along with the people in your life?"

What people? Blake had all but isolated himself—another symptom of what those terrorist fiends had stolen from him.

"Had drinks with Cole last week. And went to visit an old man in the hospital, but I knew he was unconscious."

"So why'd you go?"

Because it was easy. There were no expectations when someone was comatose.

And because he wanted help, Blake looked deeper. And deeper. As Dr. Magnum had taught him. Quieting his mind until he could work through the layers of thoughts and emotions and figure out what his psyche was telling him.

"I'd saved his life," he said slowly. "Maybe he'd

know I was there. Maybe he'd feel me somehow and reach toward me."

"Come out of the coma, you mean."

"Maybe."

"Maybe?"

Uncomfortable with her pushing, Blake nevertheless appreciated that she was only doing what it took to give him what he sought—emotional health.

"Yes," he said after another long moment. "Yes, I suppose I thought maybe my presence could bring him out of his coma."

"Because you'd bonded with him."

"I'd given him mouth-to-mouth resuscitation."

"That was a physical act, Blake. Bringing him out of his coma simply by being there suggests something else. I think we're talking about the emotions."

The impact of her words hit him hard. "I formed an emotional bond," he said, staring at her.

"Yeah."

It wasn't much in the large scheme of things, bonding with an unconscious man, but it gave him pause for thought. A big pause. And that was more than he'd had since he could remember.

Blake took with a grain of salt the rest of Dr. Magnum's reassurances that he was doing fine, that his nocturnal relapse was to be expected, a product of seeing Annie again. In the doc's world, and by her clinical definitions, he was fine. In the world that Annie inhabited, he never would be.

SHANE HAD EATEN A BROWNIE laced with methamphetamine. Though she'd worried that she was doing the right thing, Annie had called Becky, rather than the paramedics, and her friend had been able to get Shane in for an injection of a drug that reversed the effect, without the police being notified that he'd been high.

He'd have been let go as soon as they found out that the youngster hadn't been aware the potent drug was in the brownie he'd had, but still, he could have been arrested. In spite of the fact that the grandfather with whom he and his mother shared a home was the retired sheriff of River Bluff County.

"He's asleep," Becky said, joining Annie in the kitchen of the home she'd grown up in and moved back to after her divorce when Shane was two. Her father had helped the women get Shane out to the farmhouse.

Still dressed in the smock and white shoes she'd worn to work, Becky looked rumpled and exhausted. Her footsteps were heavy on the hardwood floor as she came to the table.

Her father, Hub Parker, had retreated to his large workshop out back as soon as they'd returned home from the clinic with a confused Shane in tow. Annie knew, as she was sure Becky did, that Hub wasn't angry with his grandson, or even with the kids who'd laced the brownies, but with whoever had sold them the stuff to begin with.

He'd spent his lifetime trying to keep things like

drugs and pornography out of River Bluff's schools. Out of River Bluff, period.

Annie poured her friend a glass of the herbal tea she'd brewed, and pushed a plate of ham sandwiches toward her. "I just got off the phone with Katie's parents. Apparently the brownies were brought to the park after football practice. No one knows who brought them. Katie claims she didn't eat any."

"That's convenient." The sarcasm in her friend's voice was so unlike her, Annie was worried.

She'd followed closely behind Becky all the way out to the three-bedroom white-frame farmhouse, afraid for her friend. For the thoughts she knew Becky was having; the guilt she was bearing on shoulders that were already carrying far too much.

"We got lucky, Bec. I never thought I'd hear myself say this, but thank God he went home with Katie, so he was right across the street from me, because otherwise he'd have been wandering around God knows where, and who knows who would have found him."

Plopping down in the chair next to Annie, Becky grasped her hand and gave it a squeeze. "Thank God you were there, Annie. Thank you. I don't know what I'd have done if…" Tears pooled in her eyes as she broke off.

"Hey." Flipping her hand over, Annie held on to her friend. "It's okay. You're forgetting what a small town River Bluff is. Everyone knows everyone else here. He'd have been fine."

"He could have ended up in jail, first, though."

"Not likely with Hub Parker as a grandfather," Annie said. "Those deputies would have made sure they had an airtight case before doing anything as drastic as that. And anyway, the most important thing is that he's going to be as good as new in the morning."

"Is he?" Becky's gaze flooded with worry as she glanced over. Holding her teacup with both hands, she had yet to take a sip. "He believes Katie had nothing to do with those brownies. Or the drugs."

"You don't," Annie guessed, partially because she didn't, either.

"You know her reputation. She's eighteen years old, Annie." Becky's eyes were shadowed. "What the hell does she want with my son?"

"Have you looked at Shane lately?"

"He's fifteen! Still a boy. I'll bet she's selling drugs and saw him as her next client."

"He's becoming a man, Bec," Annie said softly, compassion—and something else inexplicable, discomfiting—filling her heart. She could feel Becky's helplessness. And could see herself in the same position fifteen years hence. "You've taught him well. If that's the case, he'll make the right choice," she added.

"Unless she tempts his hormones until he's not thinking at all."

"He's your son, Bec." Annie helped herself to a sandwich, and handed one to Becky. "He's got a lot of you in him. You've set the stage, given him the tools to make the right choices."

"But what if he doesn't?"

"Then we'll be here to catch him when he falls. To pick up the pieces. And help him put his life back together again."

It sounded so easy. So…doable.

When, in fact, as Annie well knew, there were some things that just couldn't be fixed.

CHAPTER TWELVE

"SHANE NEEDS A FATHER." Becky had eaten only a couple of the finger sandwiches. But she'd finished her tea. Her expression glum, she poured herself another cup.

"He has one," Annie pointed out. When a long look was the only response forthcoming, she asked, "Does Danny know what happened today?"

"No."

"You going to tell him?"

"I suppose. Not that it will help much. We've been divorced for thirteen years. I know he worries about Shane but he has another family. Another life."

"I just thought that maybe if he knew what was going on, he could offer a little male influence in Shane's life."

"It's a little late to hope the two of them are going to bond. Besides, he's got male influence right here at home. My dad's a helluva lot better with Shane than he ever was with me."

Annie was sure Becky was right. Hub could relate to the boy. A much easier proposition than consoling a little girl who'd lost her mother.

"Maybe he just needs someone a little younger, a little more distant. A little less a retired sheriff. I can ask Cole to talk to him."

"No!" Tea splashed over the side of Becky's cup. "Please, don't say anything to your brother. Promise me, Annie."

"Okay!" She hated the fear in her friend's voice, in her wide-eyed gaze. "It really is okay, you know."

"No it's not. Cole is friends with Luke, and you know how it is with those guys. They get together and tell each other everything. They're worse than girls. Always have been." She paused, looked wildly around the kitchen, as if Luke Chisum had a direct line in from his family's ranch neighboring the Parker homestead. Becky's family's homestead.

"Luke can't hear that I'm having problems with my son. He just can't, Annie. He—"

"Bec." Annie put a hand on her friend's forearm. "It's okay. I won't say anything. You have my word on that."

Nodding, Becky took a sip of tea. And then another. "Sorry," she said with a weak grin. "I overreacted, I know. It's just, seeing Shane like that, I…"

"I know, honey. I get it."

They sat silently for a couple of minutes, each contemplating, and yet still connected.

"Have you talked to Blake yet?" Becky broke the silence between them. "About his role in this baby you want to have?"

Annie wished it wasn't so easy to follow Becky's train of thought. Wished she hadn't traveled the very same road. From Shane and Becky's issues, to hers.

"No," she said, feeling a sudden helplessness of her own.

"Don't you think you should?"

"I tried." She hated to admit that, to have out in the open how impossible a relationship between her and Blake really was. "He refused to talk about it."

"Why would he do that?"

Why did he ever? It was the one thing she'd never understood. The one thing that had broken her heart—and driven her to choose safe, comfortable, verbal Roger over Blake upon his miraculous return from the dead.

"He's the one who asked for the terms," Becky continued, frowning.

"I know." He'd asked her to marry him and be his partner forever, too. And then failed to join the partnership. "He just said to call him after I do the test."

She wanted to handle this professionally. To be unattached and grateful that she was finally going to have the baby, the family she wanted. She wanted to understand. And not to need him.

She wanted not to care.

With the weight of hopelessness dragging at her, Annie teared up again.

"Ann? Honey, how are you ever going to handle having him around for the rest of your life, visiting your son or daughter, having a say in what he or she does? How are you going to handle it when that child goes to him and he can't talk to you about it? Or even to the child?"

Blake would make a great dad. The thought sprang immediately to mind at Becky's provocation.

And then Annie considered what her friend was saying.

If Blake couldn't be there for her, he certainly wouldn't be able to be there for her child, either. A child who, as she'd been at thirteen, didn't understand that parents were people, only that when you needed them and they weren't there, you knew it had to be because of you. Because of something wrong or bad about you.

And no matter what anyone said, there was real truth to the thought. Annie might not have been the source of her father's problems, or even what drove him to take his own life. But neither had she been enough reason to keep him alive. Having her for a daughter, loving him, needing him, hadn't been reason enough for him to live.

Sick to her stomach, Annie considered what she'd done.

If she was pregnant, she'd just saddled her child with a father who couldn't tell him he loved him. It would be better for the child to have no father at all.

BLAKE PROMISED Dr. Magnum—which meant he'd promised himself—that he would not cancel his participation in Wednesday night's poker game. It might be one of those promises he wanted to keep, meant to keep, but couldn't.

Such as when he'd promised Annie he'd be home from his business trip in less than two weeks. That he'd be there for her and the baby. That there was nothing for her to be frightened of or worried about.

The way he felt when he left work, his poker promise was going to follow the way of those other unkept promises. What good would it do to present himself at the Wild Card Saloon only to have to turn around and leave again? How could that do anything but draw attention to the fact that he was not and never would be a normal human being, capable of functioning completely in society?

Tendrils of anxiety already curled through his stomach. And he was hot in the middle of San Antonio's first cold front of the season.

But he was going to River Bluff. He was going to try. Blake always tried.

And to get himself there, he'd decided to visit the Cross Fox Ranch and deliver his weanling news to Brady in person, rather than over the phone. A good feeling, not a bad one. The more he replaced bad with good, the less power the bad had to hurt him.

Rule number one of talk therapy for stress victims.

Right after the education part, where Blake learned how to identify all the things that were wrong with him—and was then told how bad it could get.

Many sufferers of PTSD were never capable of participating in a one-on-one relationship again—even in relationships that had been firmly established before the incident that precipitated the disorder.

He found Brady in the stable, shoveling muck. His friend of a little more than a year greeted him with such a sincere welcome that Blake felt a bit uncomfortable.

"I think I found you a horse." He came right to the point.

"How'd you do that? I've got fingers in channels all over the state and I've heard nothing."

"I'm not sure how," Blake answered honestly, stepping around stained straw to peak into a closed stall next to Brady. A tall chestnut mare stood there, looking bored and sad. "I have a new assistant who apparently is Wonder Man. At least to hear him tell it."

Which wasn't entirely fair. While Colin seemed to have an inordinate amount of confidence, he'd also, so far anyway, followed up every promise with action.

Blake was just finishing telling Brady about the private Henley sale when, to his surprise, Marshall Carrick stepped out of a stall at the end of the stable.

"Blake, good to see you," the older man said, coming to stand beside his son.

Shaking his hand, Blake readied himself to make his excuses and go. He'd done what he'd come to do. He'd only met the elder Carrick a few times, and while everyone thought highly of him, Blake didn't like the way the man looked at his son. As though he didn't quite trust him to carry through on what he said he was going to do.

"Blake found a weanling, Dad," Brady said, though, had Blake been in his shoes, he wouldn't have done so. Brady repeated the news, ending with, "The sale is January 16."

"Forty-five thousand, huh?"

"He'll be worth four times that after I train him," Brady said. The younger man had been trying for all of the fifteen months since Brady had returned from Vegas to get his father to take him seriously.

"Trevor Dobbs is the Cross Fox trainer," Marshall said, his voice easy, the look in his eyes not quite matching it. Marshall was a sharp businessman. Through and through.

"He's getting close to retirement."

"Try and tell him that," Marshall scoffed. "He's got another good ten years in him."

A far too generous estimate, in Blake's opinion. Dobbs had played poker with them several times since Blake's return, and he'd gathered that the other man was making plans for life after the Cross Fox.

"I'd like us to go to that sale," Brady persisted. And when he heard the "us" in that statement, Blake understood why. The ex-professional football player couldn't afford to buy the horse on his own. Blake hadn't known that until just then. Brady Carrick must have lost a hell of a lot of money during his months in Las Vegas, following his forced early retirement from the NFL.

"I appreciate your enthusiasm, son." Marshall's words were obviously sincere. "But Dobbs is doing a great job as the Cross Fox trainer. We need you right where we have you—at the front end of the Cross Fox Ranch. You might have ended your career with the Dallas Cowboys, but there are an awful lot of people who still remember you with admiration and awe. Your name and face brings us business."

"I'm more than a damn name."

Witnessing the scene, Blake wished he'd taken his leave when he'd first thought to. His friend didn't want him seeing this.

He didn't want to see it.

"You've been home, what, a year?" Marshall asked.

"Fifteen months."

"When it's been two or three times that much, we can talk," the rancher said with a pat on Brady's shoulder. "You hear some distant call, son," he continued. "I don't blame you or hold it against you, I've just learned over the years not to expect you to stick around."

"I was scouted by the Dallas Cowboys!" Brady retorted.

"And Vegas? What was that about?"

"Stupidity," he admitted, his expression faltering, leaving Blake to wonder what he wasn't saying. "A way to get lost from the fact that my life's dream had just come to an end."

Marshall seemed to remember suddenly that Blake was standing there. Or else something else occurred to him. He stood straighter, then backed away. "We'll discuss this more later," he told his son as he walked off.

Just before he was out of sight, he turned and said, "Thanks for the good work, Blake. We appreciate it."

No problem, Blake might have said if the older man had waited around for a response.

As it was, he took one look at the frustration on his buddy's face and said, "It's time for the game. You want a lift?"

Which meant that not only was he going to the game, but he was trapped into staying until the end.

Unless he found some excuse why one of the other guys would have to drive Brady home.

JUNE STOPPED BY Annie's house Wednesday evening after church, with some materials to give her daughter regarding the upcoming holiday bazaar. Annie had decided to do a series of human interest stories to garner more interest in her mother's project, to try to pull in more business for the charity function. June was collecting stories from as many of the participants as she could.

"Did you know Margie Ames started making quilts after her mother died as a way of ensuring that her memory lived on throughout Margie's life? Every single quilt she sews has at least one square of material from a piece of her mother's clothing."

Annie wasn't even sure she remembered which of her mother's peers Margie Ames was. But she wanted to know. Wanted to get reacquainted with all of the people whose stories her mom was bringing her.

She used to love to go to church. To play with the babies and hear the ladies making plans to help out someone or other, or throw a baby shower, or meet for lunch. How had she grown away from that? And why?

"Do you remember how old I was when I quit going to church?" she asked her mom, standing with her in the foyer of her home. She'd have invited her in, but didn't have a sofa to offer her a seat.

"Of course I do," June said. Though dressed as usual in nondescript, pastel-colored slacks, with a matching blouse, she had lost some weight, and she looked good. "You don't?"

Frowning when the certainty in her mother's voice made her feel as if she should know, Annie shook her head. Then tugged her little black shirt down over the waistband of her jeans, covering the thin line of belly that was showing.

"You were thirteen, Annie."

That grabbed her attention—and jabbed at her heart. "After Daddy died?"

June nodded. "You were mad at God for not saving him."

Annie had no recollection of that at all.

"Reverend Wayne tried to speak with you— several times—but you'd have none of it. You refused to go to church after that, and Cole, who'd always followed around after you, wanting to do everything you did, decided he was going to stay home with you, too."

"He did?"

With a soft smile, June nodded.

"I thought you didn't want us to go. That you left us home."

"Of course I wanted you to come to service," June said. "I hated sitting there in church by myself, surrounded by other families…."

"So why didn't you make us?"

"You were pretty feisty even back then, my dear." Her loving smile took the sting out of her words. "And I just wasn't up for the battle."

That Annie remembered. "You could have stayed home."

June shook her head, her smile fading. "Those were such hard years, honey. So many things were happening that you couldn't possibly understand. It took me years to understand them, and I was an adult. How could you possibly hope to get it?"

Things she didn't understand? Besides the fact that her father had taken his own life when he'd had an entire family who loved and supported him?

"I was just putting some tea on," she said, when she would have liked to stay right there and ask her mother what she meant. "Would you like to have some?"

With a trembling smile this time, June nodded and followed Annie back to the kitchen.

BLAKE WAS DEALING the draw just after nine Wednesday night when Cole Lawry's cell phone rang. Instantly on edge, fearing something had happened to Annie, he stopped midturn and listened.

In a matter of seconds, all of the Wild Bunch and the guests filling up the empty chairs that evening were watching Cole, listening to his end of the conversation.

And when he hung up the phone, every single man there, without saying a word, threw in his cards. The game was over for the evening.

Verne Chandler had just passed away.

"IT'S HARD TO UNDERSTAND exactly how the mind works in times of emotional stress," June was saying as her fingers played with the edge of the napkin Annie had placed by her teacup half an hour before. "Or why it's different for different people."

"But you knew what Dad did…his choice… wasn't your fault," Annie said. Even as she said the words, she was angry with herself for the double standard she'd held all these years. Her mother had been the quintessential wife, supportive through good times and bad, patient. Laughing with her husband through his good times—and supporting, encouraging him, pulling him up when he fell into the darkness.

She'd loved Annie's father with every ounce of her being.

Which was why she'd taken his death so hard.

Grieved for years, at the expense of the children he'd left behind.

Wasn't that it?

It had never occurred to Annie that her mother might have blamed herself. But why not? If a thirteen-year-old girl could take the blame, why couldn't a grown woman? One who was closest to him?

Annie had been through all the counseling. Understood that the loved ones left behind to grieve suicide victims almost always went through some stage of guilt.

So why had that never applied, in Annie's mind, to her mother?

"I assume Reverend Wayne set you straight on that," she said now, still angry. With herself. And maybe with her mother, too. Why hadn't June been home, sharing all of this with her children? Why hadn't they been able to grieve, and heal, together? As a family?

June's gaze fell, her lips straightening, as she shook her head. "Reverend Wayne was asked to leave the church, did you know that?" she murmured, seemingly from left field.

"Since he was transferred, you mean?"

"No." June looked at her, and Annie hardly recognized the steady look in her eyes. The determination. "He wasn't transferred. He was asked to leave."

"Fired?"

June nodded.

"Way back when Reverend Mary came?"

"Yes."

"Why?" Suddenly aware that she was going to hear something significant, Annie wasn't sure she was ready.

CHAPTER THIRTEEN

"WAYNE RICHARDS WASN'T a bad man," June said, and Annie instantly believed he was. Before she even knew what her mother was going to tell her. He'd brought the slump back to June's shoulders, and that was enough for Annie to dislike the man.

"What'd he do?" She couldn't wait for an answer before she said, "He didn't molest you, did he?"

"No." June's smile was bittersweet. "I almost wish he had."

"What? Why?"

"Something like that would have been easy to identify. To put a name to, to understand, to see."

"But…"

"Wayne was a power junkie." June's voice took on an odd note—one of a gentle strength, as though it had been hard-won and still wasn't sure it belonged where it had ended up. "And I was a perfect target for his addiction."

Annie poured more tea for both of them, wanting to take her mother's hand, as she had Becky's the other night, but not quite sure how to do that. How to cross the years of separation she'd erected between them.

"The more he kept me weak, the stronger he felt," June said.

"He was your counselor," Annie remembered. "You used to go see him three times a week."

"Yes, and every time I told him I thought I was ready to taper off, he'd tell me I wasn't. He'd point out weaknesses in my behavior, tell me that he was worried about you and Cole and what would happen to you if I didn't get myself under control. He told me that God was guiding him, and assured me that he'd stand right there beside me, holding my hand for as long as it took because God told him to do so. He said he had my back. When in truth he had his own. As long as I needed him, he was important."

"Damn him." The words were no less intense for their softness. Annie wanted to kill the man.

"I wish I could tell you that I caught on eventually, that I ended the sessions."

"How could you? He was your minister. A man of God. Your counselor and confidant, and he was telling you that in his professional and spiritual opinion, you were sick."

"I could have listened a little less to him and a little more to my own heart," June said.

Annie couldn't argue with that. And at the same time, she could understand how that hadn't been possible, given the circumstances. June had not only been dealing with guilt. And confusion. She'd just lost her partner. The love of her life. In a very difficult way.

"So what happened?"

"Several of the ladies in our women's circle began to get suspicious. Apparently Wayne had pulled the same thing on a mother who'd lost her child a few years before, and the poor thing ended up in a psychiatric ward. They started asking me about my sessions with him. Asked me if I'd tape one of them. I did."

"And that was it?"

"Of course not," June said, her hand shaking as she raised her cup to her lips. "It was much uglier and harder than that. We couldn't use the tape to implicate him. He didn't give me permission to tape the session, and I wasn't acting on behalf of an officer of the law. What the tape did was allow my friends to point out to me what was happening. It took a while for me to really see and believe what was going on. And another several months before I could stand before a board and go head-to-head with him, confronting him with what he'd done."

Annie was completely shocked. "You did that?"

Nodding, June didn't look up. "Hard to believe, huh?"

Annie had never disliked herself as much as she did in that moment. All the recriminations she'd heaped on her sweet mother's head. The blame for a life that wasn't as she'd expected it to be. When all the while June had been fighting an unseen battle that could have robbed her of her very ability to function.

Fighting and winning.

For herself.

And her children.

"You never said anything."

"Why would I? You and Cole had your own things to deal with. You didn't need to know how badly I'd let myself down."

Maybe not. Maybe at the time Annie had been so locked in her own grief that she wouldn't have been able to accept her mother's situation as she could now. She would probably have run scared, knowing that not only her father, but her mother, too, had deep emotional issues.

But then, who didn't? Dazed, confused, Annie sat there, processing what she'd heard. Seeing her entire life change before her eyes as she realized that she'd created a reality in her thirteen-year-old mind, one that she carried with her still, and it didn't even exist. There was no set expectation in society of what it took to be emotionally healthy. She'd only thought there was. And had spent her entire life trying to be that.

When, in truth, every single human being on the planet had emotional issues of some kind or other at some point in their lives. It was all part of the human experience.

Wasn't it?

Or was she getting this wrong, too? Justifying action to fit into some logical place? Because of some issue of her own. Some need to have everything cleanly in a place, making sense. As if she could somehow keep control of life—of the potential for pain—if she could do so.

Annie's thoughts flew all over the place, bewildering her. Was she having an epiphany? Finally coming fully to life? Or was she losing whatever hold she'd had on her mind? Was she finally losing it? Just as she'd always feared she would?

"All I ever wanted was to be a wife and mother and take care of your father and you kids," June said. "He was a good man, Annie. A loving man. He was such a gifted artist. You used to love to watch him work, do his carving. Do you remember that?"

Annie couldn't remember that at all. Could scarcely think of her father without seeing that bloodstain on the floor of the workroom out back.

"He was sick. He had a disorder that, today, they've been able to attribute to biological and physiological causes. Chromosomal imbalances, I think."

He'd been manic depressive. Annie knew that much.

"Do you ever regret marrying him?" She yearned for the answer in ways she didn't understand. "Or loving him?"

"Never." June's response was emphatic. "He had his challenges, but he loved us completely," she said. "What more could you want than that?"

Loved them completely, just not enough for the love to help him cope through the pain. And who was Annie to judge that?

How well had *she* loved? She'd certainly failed her mother.

And what about Blake? She'd turned her back on the love of her life that day he'd gotten off the airplane and literally run to her waiting arms. She'd held him then, but later that day…

"I have something I want to show you," Annie said suddenly, rising as the memories grew too vivid. Hurt too much.

She reached for June's hand, feeling at once awkward and also strangely peaceful as her mother's fingers slid easily into her own. Moving slowly, silently, she led her mom down the hall to the nursery she'd decorated.

There was going to be explaining to do. June knew nothing about Annie's plans.

But that could come. For now…

She opened the door and waited.

"Oh!" June walked over to the cradle, tears streaming down her face as she lovingly, reverently, ran her fingers along the spokes and bars of hand-carved wood. "Where did you find this?"

Annie told her about the secondhand shop outside of Waco. The day she'd gone on the Internet and researched her father's name. The picture.

"I'd never seen it before," she said. "I didn't even know he'd done cribs."

"He didn't," June said, still touching the wood as if she were touching the man who'd made it into the beautiful piece it was. "Only this one. He made it for you, but we fell on hard times and he had to sell it before you were born…."

ANNIE WASHED UP THE teacups after her mother left. Thought about baking some cookies to take into work the next day. Her boss loved chocolate chip cookies. And she wanted him in a good mood for the article she intended to propose. Something a bit more hard-hitting than positive thinking.

Mental manipulation was abusive. Widespread. And hard to identify, most particularly for the victims. It was time to shed some light on the subject. To help women like her mother, who were easy targets, women who fell prey to exploitation due to the character trait that made them special to begin with—their tenderness and their ability to trust.

The idea was only starting to take shape, but Annie had to do the piece. Maybe even try to sell it to a woman's magazine. She had a contact or two.

She didn't have any chocolate chips. But she knew Mike would let her do the article, anyway. He always did.

Wandering though her house, Annie longed for daylight and a good long bike ride. The tub invited her in for a soak. She thought about that, too, before declining. She couldn't sit still. Didn't want to be trapped in one place with her thoughts.

Was she crazy? Did she have some of her father in her, after all, and this was a low?

And sex with Blake had been the high?

Or was this merely the dark night of the soul that came before awareness? Had she been sleeping since she was thirteen, and was only now, finally, coming completely awake?

Feeling a powerful pressure to figure herself out, to know, Annie couldn't find a place to land, or anything to occupy herself with. It was too late to go out, but too early for bed. She'd only lie there and torment herself.

Hand on her lower belly, thinking of the child who would need her whole and healthy, she found herself back in the nursery—the room that, until recently, had given her all the magic in her life, the promise of good to come. It had given her a reason to get up in the morning, something to look forward to on weekends. A purpose.

Tonight, it gave her back a piece of her past. And of her future. It gave her a piece of herself.

Confused, knowing that she was on the brink of something, sensing the pain lodged in the region of her heart, Annie sat in the rocker in that beautiful room, intending to lull herself into peace with the gentle motion. But she slid down onto the floor instead. She stared at the cradle for a long time, trying to remember her father's hands as they worked the wood.

Eventually, her own hands found it, touching a spindle—tentatively at first, then lovingly, as her mother had. And her father, too?

Tim Lawry had made this bed for her. She'd paid an inordinate amount of money to buy it for her baby.

There was a message there for her. If only her mind would let her find it.

The knock on her front door wasn't as much of a surprise as it should have been. Nor was Blake's face on the other side of the screen.

She might have told herself that she wasn't

going to see him again. Wasn't going to speak to him until after she'd used the little blue stick she'd purchased the weekend before. And that communication might have just been a voice mail. Or an e-mail.

She might have told herself this, but her heart knew differently.

There was more than history and a possible fertilized egg between her and Blake. It went deeper than that. Life had something to show them. And then, perhaps, once they'd found peace in their apartness, they'd both be able to move on. Away from each other. Toward something new. Someone new.

The thought of someone out in the world someplace, just waiting for Annie to find him, moved her not at all.

But she clung to it just the same as she opened her door to the man she'd lost her heart to so long ago. It was time to take it back.

"I OWE YOU SOMETHING," Blake said from the other side of the door.

Annie nodded, stood aside for him to come in.

Still dressed in slacks and a white business shirt, Blake looked tired as he stood in her foyer, but Annie couldn't offer him a seat at the kitchen table. It was too warm and friendly, too familylike.

Instead, waiting for him to state his business, she wrapped her arms around herself. She wasn't going to make a mistake here, lose herself through a lack of self-control. She wasn't going to be physically weak, give in to the temptation he posed, standing there so real and warm and…all that was Blake.

"I love you, Annie."

She fell back against the wall. Stared at him. Waited for something else, an indication of what he'd really said, since she'd obviously transposed her own hallucinations on top of his message.

"I've always loved you."

He did. He had. Frightened, Annie leaned there, watching him. Was he going to sprout wings, too? Or propose to her?

Could she stay in this state of self-delusion forever? If she spoke to him would he disappear? Or would he be telling her that he was sorry for not loving her and that he never wanted to see her again?

The sadness in his eyes was not indicative of a man in love. Professing his love.

"This doesn't change anything," he continued into her silence. "I have no interest in a relationship of any kind—other than to be a presence in my child's life, if, indeed, there is a child."

So he was still on board with that. Annie clung to the one thing she seemed able to grasp.

He appeared to be awaiting a response. "Okay." It seemed appropriate, given her understanding of the situation—which was slim to none.

"Okay, then." He turned to go.

She couldn't let him do that. Straightening, she called, "Blake?"

"Yeah?" He stopped at the door, turned.

"Thank you."

"For what?"

"Telling me."

He nodded. "I'm just sorry that I didn't do so six years ago. You should have heard it then."

"I'm glad I'm hearing it now." He'd said he loved her. Blake had told her he loved her. And he was walking out the door?

"Would you like a glass of wine? Or tea or something?"

Hesitating, with his hand on the door, he seemed about to say something more, and then just nodded, following her down the hall to the kitchen.

She opened a bottle, poured two glasses and carried them over to the table.

As if he hadn't slept in weeks, Blake dropped into a chair. Sipped his wine. Rubbed his eyes.

"Verne Chandler died tonight."

"He did?" Cole hadn't called. "I'm really sorry to hear that."

"When he didn't regain consciousness, they figured it was coming."

Cole had called the day before and had told her the same thing. Jake's uncle had spent too many years living hard for his body to have the capacity to fight back.

"They said his liver was hardly functioning at all. If he'd lived he'd have needed a transplant."

"Judging from what I saw of the man around town, he didn't look in good enough health to survive surgery like that."

"Probably not."

Blake seemed to be taking the whole thing so personally. "You did all you could, Blake. You gave him a fighting chance. Probably his only chance."

"I know." Still, his eyes were shadowed.

"So what happens next? No one knows where Jake is. What if the authorities can't locate him?"

"I suspect they will. They've got sources you and I don't have access to."

"And the body just waits until they do?"

Blake shrugged. "My guess is the sheriff will find Jake pretty quickly now that they have a good reason to do so. Cole asked to be the one to call him."

That wasn't going to be easy. But she respected her brother for making that effort, especially considering how hurt he had been by Jake's failure to ever contact him over the years, leaving his best friend in the dust, just as he had the town that had scorned him. "Are they going to let him?"

"Yeah."

His wineglass half-empty, Blake didn't appear to have anything else to say. Or be in any hurry to leave. She'd never seen him like this. Didn't know what to make of any part of the visit.

"Why'd you come here tonight, Blake?" She didn't want to open the door to anything more personal between them. The question came, anyway.

His perusal was completely personal. And weighty.

"For you," he said finally. "I've had a lot of time to…think."

The conversation was not easy for him. Sensing

the effort it was taking Blake to sit there and attempt to engage with her in this way, Annie felt like crying.

"And I can see how my reticence hurt you. I never meant to hurt you, Annie."

"I know. I never thought I could hurt you, either, but then I did."

He didn't seem inclined to say anything more. And Annie felt as if they'd only just begun to scratch the surface of all that needed to be said.

"I always thought that love would be enough," she murmured, almost to herself, replaying not only her relationship with Blake, but the conversation she'd had with her mother. "Yet sometimes it's just not, is it?"

"No." Blake stood. "Sometimes it's just not." He took his glass to the sink. Rinsed it and put it in the dishwasher, loading it exactly as she would have done. But then, he'd know how she loaded the dishwasher. They'd done it together hundreds of times.

He was going to leave her. She knew that had to happen. That for them to consider any alternative would only bring more pain to both of them.

And tonight she wasn't herself. She was changing right before her eyes. Wasn't sure who that self was going to turn out to be.

Tonight she didn't have any rules.

"Blake?" She spoke to his back for the second time in half an hour.

"Yeah?"

He didn't turn. And Annie couldn't wait. Close behind him, she slid her arms around his middle, pulling him back against her. Laying her head on his stiff back, she began to caress him, tentatively at first, and then, when he moved and she feared he was going to pull away, to leave, she dropped her hand down to the part of him that had been reserved for only her at one point in his life. Just for tonight, she wanted it to be for her again.

"Please?"

With a groan, Blake turned, slid his arms beneath her and carried her in to the bed.

CHAPTER FOURTEEN

THE ONLY WAY TO HEAL was to understand the disorder, recognize the challenges and face them headon. Blake recited words from his counselor as he sat in the Lincoln on Friday night, once again heading back to River Bluff.

Not to see Annie. He'd meant what he'd said about that. He was never again going to allow himself to consider a relationship with her. He loved her too much, and whomever he was with was going to be hurt by his PTSD. Statistically, that was a given.

But that didn't mean he wasn't going to do all he could to heal. Barely aware of the trees, the grass and rolling grazing lands as his expensive car purred down the road, Blake thought of the child he might have—Annie's child—and knew that he would push himself every day to overcome the effects of the anxiety-ridden condition that plagued him.

He was not going to live side by side with Annie, grow old with her. But they would share a child—a part of him and a part of her together forever—and for that he would be grateful. Thankful. Happy.

In the meantime, despite a strong inclination to go home and stay there for the weekend, he'd accepted an invitation from Cole to watch the *Godfather* and share a pizza. He'd never seen the famous movies, and Cole was constantly quoting from them. "Taking it to the mattresses" his friend said when the going got tough and he refused to give up.

All Blake could think about when he heard those words was Annie.

Cole had been after him for months to join him for a movie fest. So here Blake was, taking another step out, pushing himself to live. For Annie's baby.

Since his divorce, Cole had devoted his evenings and weekends to finishing his house. He was far from finished. Nothing much on the walls, the place was devoid of furniture, too, except for a large-screen television and the pair of black leather recliners his ex hadn't wanted.

Downing his first beer more quickly than normal, Blake focused almost completely on breathing, relaxing, repeating mantras that Dr. Magnum had taught him. He was sitting down to watch three movies about organized crime. There would be violence.

But they were only flicks. Fiction.

He'd never been the victim of physical violence.

"Any word on Jake?" he asked his friend as they waited for the pizza to be delivered.

Shaking his head, Cole opened a second beer for himself and poured a quarter of it down his throat before dropping into a reclining chair next to Blake. They sat right in front of the screen, which was playing, and replaying, the opening sequence of the DVD.

"He wasn't at the last known address. The sheriff says it could take a day or two to hear back, since it's not an emergency. They're looking for a social security match on other records."

Surprising himself with the extent of his curiosity over the absent Wild Bunch original, and Cole's best childhood friend, Blake asked, "Where was that address?"

"Someplace in California."

"Is that where he went when he left here?"

Cole tipped the bottle to his lips again. "I have no idea." There was more than a hint of attitude in his response.

"He didn't even tell you that much?"

"Nope." Another sip, and Cole held the dark glass bottle against the leg of his jeans. "Fifteen years of friendship and he just up and left. Didn't even tell me he was going."

"And he's never called."

"Nope."

"You sure he wasn't abducted? It happens, you know."

"I'm sure. He took everything he cared about. Which wasn't all that much. And left a note for Verne, telling him to do whatever he wanted to with the Wild Card."

"Did Verne ever hear from him again?"

"Not so's he ever said. But who knows with Verne? He had a hard time remembering if he'd had breakfast on any given day."

Yes, and there but for the grace of God went Blake. He took another sip of beer, knowing that he'd have his limit and be done. While the immediate relief alcohol brought might be welcome, the long-term effects were not.

He had a life to think about. Maybe more than one, if Annie's test on Tuesday was positive.

"From what I've gathered, the people in this town gave Jake a hard time while he was growing up."

"He brought it on with his devil-may-care attitude," Cole said, and then softened. "It was all a cover-up, though. Jake was a great guy. The best. He just couldn't get a break. He was a bastard and his old lady was the town's barmaid. Growing up in the back of the bar… The things that guy heard and saw made the rest of us drool, even in the retelling."

It couldn't have been easy, Blake figured, being so different in such a small town. He'd struggled a time or two with his own untraditional upbringing, with fitting in and feeling like a normal kid during those insecure adolescent years, and he'd lived in a town where you didn't even know the people who lived in the condo above you.

"I think what did him in was falling for Rachel Diamonte. Her father, Mike Diamonte, owned quite a successful spread just outside of town. It was a classic heartbreak waiting to happen, boy from the wrong side of the tracks in love with one of the beautiful rich girls."

"Did she like him?"

"Seemed to. But when he finally got up the guts to ask her out, she said no. He saw her alone once more after that, in the pecan grove by the bar. He never told me what happened, but I gathered it ended badly."

"Whatever happened to her?"

"Last I knew, she'd married, was living in Chicago and was expecting a baby."

"Are her folks still around?"

Cole shook his head and emptied his bottle of beer. "Mike died about five years ago. His wife, Sarah, sold the ranch. Moved into an elite development in River Bluff."

"You're doing a good job on this place," Blake said next, looking around.

"It's coming. But slowly."

"Need some help? I got time this weekend."

Cole was in the middle of enthusiastically accepting the offer when the doorbell rang.

Dinner had arrived.

SONNY CORLEONE WAS a hothead. A concern, considering that, as the eldest son of Don Vito Corleone, the godfather, he was next in line to run the family. And take on responsibility for handling many millions of dollars in businesses, as well as managing politicians and hit men.

With his last bottle of beer just started, Blake pushed back in the lounger. He was replete with pizza. Enjoying comfortable, nonthreatening companionship that demanded nothing of him, and an interesting film. He was good. Better than good. He was fine.

A few scenes back, when Sonny had started beating up Carlo, husband to Sonny's sister Connie, for roughing her up, Blake had had a moment of discomfort. But that had turned out to be nothing more than the normal adrenaline rush that came with experiencing something secondhand.

Alone when another call came through, Sonny heard that Carlo was at it again. That Connie was being brutalized. And with the famous *Godfather* theme playing in the background, Sonny rushed to his sister's rescue. Disregarding his father's orders that he go nowhere, ever, without his entourage of bodyguards, he blew out into the streets in his big black car. If he lost even a second, it might cost Connie her life.

He was going to show that bastard what happened to a man who disrespected his women. He was going to beat the pulp out of him. He was going to make him pay for what had been done to his sister.

Reading all of this in the man's expression, Blake was there with Sonny, determined to set the world right for his woman. Sometimes there were just things a man had to do—regardless of what he'd been told. And taught. Sonny might have a temper, but this time it was serving him in good stead.

He was a big brother going to the rescue. A knight in shiny black armor.

Reaching the entrance to the gated community where Connie and Carlo lived, Sonny skidded to a halt at the closed gate. It didn't open. He pulled up to the gatehouse, ready to drive through the damn thing if he couldn't get a response at once.

Hurry, Blake urged silently. Every second of hell for Connie, for the victim, was another infusion of stress, another series of memories, another level of walls being built to endure—walls that would imprison you forever, if they became too thick. If you needed them for too long.

If there was so much pain that you couldn't cope with it anymore.

Men appeared on either side of Sonny's car. There was one moment of shocked recognition. Blake could still see the streets of Jordan outside the restaurant where he'd been eating. And then, in his peripheral vision, they were there again, those men on the screen, coming up on both sides of him. Dressed in black, with hoods and rifles.

Shots fired. Hundreds of them. Sonny's car was riddled with bullet holes, so many the car would never be the same. His body jerked, again and again, one way and another, as the slugs hit their mark, some tearing clear through him. Some lodging inside.

Blake could feel the burning against his wrists. Down his lungs, inside his diaphragm, as they poured something down his throat. Something touched the back of his head. He had to swat it off, to push and shove and get away, but he couldn't move. There were too many of them, and every one of them had a vise grip on his body, hauling him away in plain sight of the other patrons in the restaurant.

Not one of whom said a word.

He was going to die. That was inevitable. His body would be found slumped over, bloody, beaten to an unrecognizable pulp. As with another body he'd seen. Annie would come to identify him and she'd be unable to do so. His baby was not going to know his father.

With strength that came from someplace deep inside him, from the source of all power, he struck out at the chains that bound him, the thugs who, right then, were dragging him God knew where.

He couldn't see. All was black. There was something over his head, suffocating him.

His skin burned. His throat burned. Oh, God, he couldn't save himself. He'd promised Annie, and now he was being dragged like a sack of garbage, and he couldn't stop them. His arms were jerked behind him, his wrists cuffed. Pain seared through his shoulder sockets, his collarbone. A blow to the chest and all he knew was red-hot agony.

No! He tried to scream, but no sound came out. He tried again and again. Needed someone to see him. To see what was happening to him. To give him just a chance at saving himself.

Another blow—to the stomach. More pain. He was going to puke…

"Blake…"

They knew his name. How in the hell did they know his name? He'd been held captive in a hellhole for four years and had never once heard his name spoken.

"Blake?" Another hand on him, on his shoulder, gripping him. He swung with enough force to break the bonds holding him, to bust the cuffs right off his wrists. The pain of their letting loose tore into his skin, burning. Always burning. He swung again. Connected. To flesh. Thank God.

He could hit. Blow after blow flew from him. Hitting air, but at least they'd let go of him.

"Blake. Come on, man. Calm down. Becky's on her way over. And Annie, too. It's okay. You're going to be okay…."

The voice continued to talk to him as he fought. Almost continuously mentioning Annie. How she was driving her car instead of riding her bike. She'd be here in moments.

They were bringing Annie. It was a lie. Another cruel taunt. Another bit of manipulation meant to make him beg. To howl with misery. They took pleasure in making him cry.

They knew about Annie.

How could they know about Annie?

He had to stop. To think. If they touched him again, he'd fight some more. He was ready. Shaking, he held his arms out, waiting. Thinking. Always trying to think. To outthink. To maintain ownership of his own thoughts, rather than falling prey to theirs.

"Where is he?"

They had a tape of Annie's voice? No, wait. He was sitting on something soft. And had clothes. He was wearing long pants.

"Blake?" Annie's voice was beside him. He was hearing things again. For so many years he'd heard that voice, only to open his eyes and find himself alone in a cramped and cold cement hole. If he looked at himself, he'd see his naked torso, the too skinny legs and scabbed stomach—the unhealed sores from lying on the cold cement. He'd see bare feet—and on good days, a torn, dirty cloth covering his loins.

If he opened his eyes.

Shivering, Blake lay there, willing Annie's voice to continue. Every second he could hold on to the sound of her was one less second of hell. Not daring to move, knowing that even the slightest motion would bring back the cold, hard floor, he remained inert. A skill he'd perfected during his captivity.

"Blake?"

Her voice again. Her sweet voice. If he could just hang on to it long enough to fall asleep…

The loud noise jerked him upright. A gunshot? Had they shot someone else? Like a game of Russian roulette, their captors had arbitrarily chosen members of their group to execute. The dead would be paraded past every hole, every captive made to look, knowing that he might be next.

"Hey, Blake, it's Becky. How you doing?"

Becky? That was a new one. Becky who? The only Becky he knew was Annie's friend. Had they taken her, too?

"I'm just going to touch your hand, Blake." The voice came again. "Just to feel your pulse. Can I do that?"

They knew damn well, no matter what voice they used, that they could do anything they pleased with him. He was their property. Their toy. They could strip him naked, lay him out spread-eagled on a table, tie his hands and legs, shine a bright light on his body and laugh at him.

He waited, closing his mind off, only half wondering what means of humiliation they'd use this time.

"Talk to him, Annie."

"I'm here, Blake. Becky's going to feel your pulse, okay?"

There it was again. If he could just hold on to Annie's voice...

He moved his hand, and found fingers clutching it. He'd have to let Annie go soon. He couldn't take her with him to the places they took him. Couldn't have her see or know...

"You're safe. We're all here with you." He still heard her.

The fingers moved to his wrist.

Don't go, Annie. Please don't go.

"His pulse is high, but not alarmingly so. It's slowing down now."

"Cole's here. And me. And Becky…"

His hand was gently placed back at his side. On the softness of fabric. Fabric. He had clothes on.

He…

Oh, God.

He was in Cole Lawry's living room.

He'd had an episode. One of the worst he'd had in more than eighteen months.

And everyone had seen it. If he opened his eyes they'd be there, staring at him. Knowing.

Trapped in an entirely new kind of hell, Blake considered his options.

And because he was Blake, because he was a man who didn't run, who didn't shy away from the hard work, who only shied away from hurting those he cared about, he did what any man in his position would do.

He fell asleep.

"Okay, so tell me what's going on."

Dressed in jeans, a short white top and the sweater she'd pulled on just before she'd run out the door, Annie sat at Cole's kitchen table with her brother and Becky, drinking cups of the too-strong coffee Cole had brewed.

She and Cole both looked to Becky, who was holding her cup with both hands. Annie couldn't look at the bruise on her brother's cheek. It scared her to death.

"I can't give an official diagnosis, of course," Becky said. "But from what I know about Blake's history and from what I've seen tonight, I'd say he suffers from post-traumatic stress disorder."

"What does that mean, specifically?" Cole asked. "I know the basic parameters, the stuff everyone knows. But not like this. How often does it happen? Will he always go through this? Isn't there anything anyone can do to help him?"

Annie's heart froze in fear as Cole's questions came pouring out.

"I can't answer you, Cole," Becky said, frowning. "Not specifically. As far as I know, every case is different. But generally speaking, it all depends."

"On what?" Annie leaned forward, looking to her friend for honesty.

"How much he suffered when he was there. What, exactly, they did to him…"

"He said there was no physical abuse. I assumed that meant he was treated okay, but just not free to leave."

"Maybe. But with what I just saw in there, I'd say no."

"So what was that in there?" Cole was on his second cup of coffee.

Unable to sit still, filled with an uncomfortable energy she didn't entirely understand, Annie paced to the door of the kitchen, peeking in on Blake in the next room, just to reassure herself he was really asleep.

And sleeping peacefully.

"One of the major symptoms of PTSD is reliving traumatic events. We all have memories and are sometimes attacked by them, but in Blake's case, he relives the bad event in real time. Experiencing every nuance of it exactly as if it's happening again."

"He kept calling for Annie."

"I'm guessing he did that a lot while he was gone. Probably anytime things got to be too much for him."

"So he just goes through life spacing out periodically? Thrashing about without knowing what he's doing?" Annie stood beside Becky's chair, angry as hell, as if her friend could do something about all of this.

"No." Becky's voice was calm in a way she didn't usually speak to Annie. Calm, as if she was dealing with a patient. "Something must have triggered it," she said. "And I'm guessing, if you could get Blake to talk to you about it, he'd be able to tell you exactly what it was. PTSD is largely manageable, if certain conditions are met."

Now that's what Annie needed to hear. Her heart was breaking for this man. For what he'd suffered. And continued to suffer. Blake was a good man. The best. He didn't deserve any of this. "What conditions?"

"Early intervention helps tremendously," Becky said. "If Blake sought help when he was released, he's probably got this under control most of the time. And based on the fact that he and Cole are close friends and Cole knew nothing about it, and also based on the fact that he runs a successful business, I'd say that was probably the case."

"You think he's in counseling?"

"He'd pretty much have to be. He also might be on medication."

"For what?"

"Anxiety. Depression. Those are the most common side effects. Maybe some kind of sleep aid."

"Sleep aid? He didn't have a whit of trouble falling asleep," Cole interjected. His face was still unnaturally pale. His mouth was pinched, as if he was feeling sick.

"For someone with PTSD there are usually three areas of trouble. The first, you saw tonight. The second is called avoidance. It's the need to keep yourself from anything that might trigger a memory—an episode like you just saw. It also often creates a kind of void, an emotional numbness, in the victim."

So much was starting to make sense.

"And the third?" Annie asked.

"It encompasses several things, the most common of which is insomnia or some other form of sleep disorder."

Could that be why Blake had left her bed each night after making love? Not to abandon her, and not because he didn't want to stay, but because he was afraid to? Because he knew he might not be able to control what happened if he fell asleep?

Her eyes filling with tears, Annie thought about

what she'd seen tonight. She hated what she was hearing.

And loved Blake Smith with all her heart. His pain was hers. His suffering was hers.

And his challenges would be hers, too. Whether he agreed to share his life with her or not.

She was irrevocably in love with him. When he suffered, so would she.

And as she dozed in the lounger in Cole's living room that night, staying right next to Blake, needing to be close to him, she understood two very important things.

She knew why June Lawry had said she'd have married Tim all over again, if she'd been given the chance. And Annie knew, too, that she had to forgive her father for taking his own life.

Just as she absolutely could not—and did not—blame Blake for reliving a traumatic event, she couldn't blame her father for having an imbalance that made his pain unendurable.

Both men needed to be loved. Cherished. Not condemned.

CHAPTER FIFTEEN

THE LAST THING BLAKE expected to see when he woke up in the early hours of Saturday morning was Annie, sleeping in the chair beside him. His last rational recollection was of Cole sitting there.

The television was off, the house quiet. His buddy must have gone up to bed.

And Becky? Had she been there? Or had he dreamed that part?

He'd had an episode. He knew that. Recognized the feeling of emptiness that always came after one of them. The feeling that he'd passed out and lost part of his life. He'd only had a few full-out attacks, but all it took was one to know what had happened.

He'd pushed himself too hard. Was too impatient. And stupid, too, to try to prove to himself that there was nothing wrong with him.

There was no way, as tired as he was, as much as he was hurting for Annie, as often as he'd been reliving their marriage—and the way it had fallen apart—that he'd been in any state to watch a violent movie.

He'd known better.

Glancing at his watch, seeing that it was only three in the morning, Blake rose slowly from the chair. Reached for the keys he'd dropped on the table beside him. Slipped into the loafers he'd worn to work the day before. If he was careful, he could be home before either Annie or Cole woke up.

"Hold it right there, cowboy."

Still lying back in the opposite chair, Annie was staring straight at him, wide-awake.

Hand hovering over his keys, Blake froze.

"Where do you think you're going?"

"Home."

"Not tonight you aren't. It's an hour and a half drive."

"It's an hour with no traffic, Annie, and I've done it hundreds of times. You know that."

"Not after going through what you went through tonight."

His heart sank. Blake dropped into the chair, staring at the darkened room. He might have had a waking nightmare earlier, but it was no comparison to the living nightmare he was having now.

Annie knew.

"You were here," he said. He'd been hoping that her voice had been part of the illusion. It always had been in the past.

"Just at the end."

Like that made it any better. From what he'd read and understood, from what he'd been told, these occurrences were all the same from beginning to end.

Humiliated at the thought of Annie seeing him thrashing about like a wild man, at the very idea that she would ever know the things he saw inside when these things happened, Blake was pretty certain his life had reached an all-time low.

"It's okay, Blake. No one holds it against you. We just want to help."

"I don't need any help." That much was true. As long as he helped himself.

"Becky was here, did you know that?"

He grunted.

"She explained a lot of things to Cole and me."

Blake listened as his beautiful ex-wife reiterated points he'd read—and heard—hundreds of times. And in the end, though still humiliated, he was at least impressed with Becky's accuracy.

"I want to help, Blake," Annie said again. "Becky says you obviously used thoughts of me as a coping tool during your captivity."

No longer so impressed, Blake wished the other woman had minded her own business. Deciding the best defense was silence, he didn't respond.

"That being the case, I can help now, too," she said. "If I give you a sense of peace, it stands to reason that you'd have fewer episodes if I were—"

"No." He couldn't sit here and listen to this. Couldn't even consider the idea of Annie in his life on a personal basis. "You don't bring me peace." He hadn't meant to be so harsh, but he had to put a stop to this. Now. "You coming back into my life has brought on these episodes."

Annie's gasp brought him to his senses. Told him that he'd just said something he was going to regret for the rest of his life. He'd hurt her again. In an attempt to save her from hurt.

"It's not as bad as it seems," he said, choosing his words with more care. "Most of the time life sails on with relative normality."

As long as he kept all his safety measures in place.

"Becky said with early intervention you could overcome, or at least completely manage, the disorder."

"She's right."

"Did you have that?"

"Yes." And because he was sorry he'd hurt her, because he knew that words were important to Annie, he continued. "Education goes a long way toward instilling managing skills, as well."

"What about medication? Do you take anything to help?"

"Not really. A minimum-dosage sleeping pill every six months or so."

"And you've really only had a few of these things, these episodes, in over two years' time?"

"Really." If you didn't count his night stalker visits. And he wasn't.

"So what you're telling me is that you've got this pretty much under control."

Her hair, tousled around her face and shoulders, made him want to bury his fingers in it, in her. To get lost in Annie's arms and never find his way out.

"Pretty much."

"So what set you off tonight? Besides me, that is."

"I shouldn't have said that Annie. I'm sorry." He couldn't really see her expression in the darkness, couldn't see her eyes, but he could tell they were glistening.

"Of course you should, if it's the truth."

"It's not what you think."

"It's okay, Blake. I understand."

"No," he interrupted. "I don't think you do. It's not you who's caused the resurgence of stress," he told her. "It's staying *away* from you that does that."

"Then…"

"No, Annie. I am not in the market for a relationship. And if you weren't feeling sorry for me, you'd admit that neither are you. We just had this conversation. Remember?"

"People change, Blake."

"Overnight?"

"Sometimes."

Painfully equipped with far more information than Annie had on this subject, Blake wasn't going to entertain any such ideas. Period.

"So what precipitated tonight's troubles?"

Welcoming the change of topic, he told her about the scene in the movie, the violence. Realizing that he wasn't in any state to have taken it on.

"So you identified with Sonny's situation, and that's all it took," Annie said.

"Tonight, yes. Generally, I can see it coming and focus on something else enough to ward off any adverse reaction."

"Tell me what you saw tonight, Blake. Tell me what happened to you over there."

His mind blank, Blake stared in her direction, mouth open but with nothing to say. Not a word occurred to him.

"Please?"

What could he give her? Running through his mind in search of any tidbit he might share, Blake couldn't find a thing.

"I…can't, Annie. I just can't."

She didn't press him. With a small, stiff nod, she let him off the hook.

"Thank you."

Her head turned toward him. "For what?"

"Understanding."

She smiled then, something more than mere politeness. "I care, Blake, and I always want to under—stand. Don't you get that, yet?"

He couldn't let himself "get it." The temptation to take the precious gift she was offering would be too great. And that would be the greatest travesty of all.

Annie's need for love and his disorder. A match made in hell.

ON MONDAY, Cole called Blake to tell him that the sheriff had phoned with a current address and phone number for Jake Chandler. Wade Barstow had known someone, who knew someone, and they were able to speed up the process of tracing him through a cell phone bill.

"How did he take the call?" Blake asked his

friend, really wanting to know how *Cole* had handled the conversation. Whether he'd ever openly acknowledge it or not, Cole had been greatly hurt by his friend's disappearance.

"He hasn't taken it yet." Cole sounded frustrated. "His voice mail says he's out of the country for a few days. He's due back at the end of the week."

"Did you leave a message?"

"No, I didn't figure this was the kind of thing you left on a machine."

"You didn't even ask him to call you?"

"Nope." Cole's defenses were definitely in high gear, leaving Blake to wonder why he'd asked to make this particular call. The local police would have been happy to pass along the job to the police department in the town where Jake Chandler lived. "Didn't want to give him a chance to ignore the message," Cole finally admitted.

At which time, Blake decided that maybe he didn't like Jake Chandler all that much.

ANNIE WAS UP EARLY Tuesday morning. Much earlier than usual. She'd been awake, on and off, since the middle of the night—and she was restless about what was to come.

Early morning was the best time to test. And today was the day.

At six, while it was still dark outside, and when she normally would have been sound asleep, she slid out of her narrow bed, intending to head straight to the bathroom, get the deed done and crawl back under her blankets.

Hopefully to sleep. For hours and hours. Forever, if that's what it took to escape the pain of loving Blake. Worrying about him. Understanding that too much stood between them for them to make each other happy.

On her way to the bathroom, she stopped off at the living-room window, stood gazing out into the deserted street, looking up and down for any homes that might have lights on. Weren't there kids who needed to be ready for school? Lunches to make? Men who had the long drive into San Antonio to work? Surely someone besides her was up and about.

Surely they were, just not within view of Annie's front window.

But wait, was that movement out there? Certain she'd seen something, she leaned closer to the glass, studying the darkness, trying to focus just beyond where she'd noticed the motion, hoping to bring it more clearly into view.

Minutes later, when nothing further appeared, she relaxed. She'd best get the test kit out before she called the cops over trees rustling in the wind. Get back to being herself.

As if she'd ever be herself again, should that little strip of paper change color.

With a hand on her stomach, which had been finding its way there a lot lately, Annie stared out into the street, trying to imagine how she was going to feel if she knew that she was pregnant with Blake's baby.

And how she would feel if she wasn't.

Either way, there were things to fear. And reasons to rejoice. If she wasn't pregnant, she'd have a reason to get Blake to sleep with her again—another shot at convincing him to stay with her.

And if she was, if she had his baby inside her already, growing, a product of her and Blake, of a love they shared, even if they couldn't embrace it fully in their lives, then she would be complete in a way she hadn't been for far too long.

Only then could she let go of her grief over the past, and move on to the future.

Only then…

She saw the movement again. And this time, she *really* saw it. Over by the window on the south side of Katie Hollister's home. If Annie wasn't mistaken, and she knew she wasn't, it was at Katie's bedroom window. Someone was climbing out. Straightening up. Looking around furtively before heading down the street.

Someone who'd crawled in that window twenty minutes before, when Annie had thought she'd seen something?

Someone who looked alarmingly like Becky's son, Shane.

SHE WAS WRONG. She had to be wrong. She was definitely wrong. But just to be sure, Annie grabbed her phone and dialed Becky's cell phone. Her friend always had it with her at night, in case of emergency. She turned it to Vibrate, so it wouldn't wake her father or Shane if it rang.

"Annie? Are you…?" Becky sounded wide-awake.

Much more so than Annie felt. "What?"

"You were getting up at six to do the test. Was it positive?"

She'd actually forgotten, for the moment. "I haven't done it yet."

"You need a pep talk, first? You want me to come over and sit with you, while you wait for the results?"

"I need you to go check Shane's bedroom."

"Why?" Becky's entire tone changed.

"Just do it, please?"

There were shuffling sounds in the background—Becky taking her phone with her down the hall to her son's bedroom. Annie counted to ten. And then again. *Please let him be there,* she prayed. *Let him—*

"He's in his bed—" Becky's whisper broke off. "No he's not. His pillows are tucked under the covers, to make it look like a body's there."

Damn.

Damn. Damn. Damn.

"What do you know, Ann?" Becky asked, all business and strength for the moment.

"I just saw him climb out of Katie Hollister's bedroom window."

"You think he's sleeping with her? He's only fifteen years old!"

"I don't know what to think," Annie said quickly, more worried about a drug buy than sex at the moment. "What are you going to do now?"

"Sit right here and wait for him to sneak back in."

Annie would like to be a fly on the wall for that one. "And then what?"

"I have no idea. I'm hoping something comes to me between now and then."

"Be firm with him, Bec. Don't go feeling sorry for him because he doesn't have a father there with him."

"I know. I won't."

"And don't let him give you any guff. He might have grown taller than you this past year, but you're still the boss there."

"I know."

"You going to tell your dad?"

"Who knows? Probably. But not until after I hear what Shane has to say."

"I love you."

"I know, Annie. I love you, too."

"Call me as soon as you're done, okay? Sooner, if you need me."

"Okay, I will. Thanks, Annie, you're the best."

"So are you, my friend. So are you."

Annie rang off and headed back to the bathroom. There was no time like the present to see if her future was going to be anything like Becky's.

BLAKE CLOSED THE CONDO deal over breakfast, at eight o'clock Tuesday morning. In spite of the fact that he'd looked at his watch every other minute. Annie should have called by now.

Was he going to be a father or wasn't he?

And if not, was he going to try with her again, or leave well enough alone?

He was meeting a prospective client, a referral from Colin, at ten. Should he phone her before then, or continue to wait for her call?

Why hadn't she called already? Because she'd had bad news? Or good? Or had something prevented her from taking the test at all?

When he realized that he had no idea at this point whether or not Annie would find a positive test good news or bad, Blake put his cell phone back in the case resting against his hip, picked up his briefcase and headed to his next appointment. He had a business to run. A life to live.

Annie would phone him when she was ready.

BLAKE DIDN'T HEAR from Annie all day. For a good part of the time he managed to keep his mind under control, in order to focus on the business at hand. He'd had a lot of practice at it.

But by late that afternoon, he'd run out of self-control. He tried several times to reach her, and when she didn't pick up, he finally dialed Cole, who hadn't heard from his sister in two days.

"How you doing, buddy?" Cole asked, as he had each day since Friday night's episode, managing to find various pressing reasons to call.

"Good. Yourself?" Blake asked.

"All right. Ron was after me about joining the game tomorrow night."

"So invite him. We work around him."

"My mother's trying to rope me into building a new dais for Santa for the church bazaar next month."

"Remind me to stay away from June!"

"Yeah," Cole grunted. "So, you're good?"

"I'm fine, Cole." If he hadn't been so uncomfortable with the attention, Blake would have been amused. "Really. It's under control."

"You're sure?"

"I'm sure. Just sorry as hell I caught your face. How's the shiner?"

"Gone. Wasn't much. And I was a fool for getting in your way," Cole said. "It was clear you weren't there. I don't know what I was doing."

"You were trying to help."

And that was precisely why Blake had to live alone. He'd slugged his best friend. It made him sweat, to think of the damage he could have done. What if it had been Annie? Or, God forbid, their child? What if he'd broken Cole's nose? Or done more serious damage?

"Becky said you probably saw the symptoms coming."

"I pushed myself too hard."

"And if it hadn't been just me, if there'd been someone else around, someone you might, say, hurt with your superior strength, you would have made different choices about pushing so hard."

Of course. He managed responsibly....

Blake's thoughts froze.

"You've been talking to Annie," he said, half accusation and half...he didn't know what.

"She believes that you plan to live alone the rest of your life because of this thing. Because you're afraid of what you might do."

"Wouldn't you be?"

"Depends."

"On what?"

"How well you manage yourself. What control you've been able to gain over it. How often these episodes happen. How much it actually affects your ability to be productive every day."

"One episode could be all it takes."

"So could an explosion with my gas grill. Or a car accident. Does that mean you'll never drive anyone?"

Cole didn't understand. The ramifications of living as he did weren't something anyone could understand if he hadn't been there....

"Let me ask you this." Cole was in one of his irritatingly positive, dog-with-a-bone modes. "What does your doctor say about your chances of having a relatively normal family life?"

Blake's sessions with Dr. Magnum were confidential.

"Have you asked her?"

"Yes."

"And?"

It didn't matter what she said. She wouldn't have to live with any consequences.

"Blake?"

"She sees no reason whatsoever that I can't marry and raise a family." He bit out the words. They were like salt in a wound. Because no matter what the doctor thought, if Blake didn't believe it, then nothing else mattered.

BLAKE WAITED ANOTHER half hour. Called Annie four times more, and then called Becky. He didn't know her. Had to look up her number in the phone book. Other than the one night, he'd probably never even been around her—unless she'd been in the diner on some poker night when he'd stopped to eat.

But Cole had spoken of her so often, in reference to Annie, that he felt as if he knew her. More importantly, he knew how well she knew Annie.

"Blake? Is something wrong? You need help?" Annie's friend asked as soon as he'd identified himself, her voice filled with concern.

And sympathy… Which was one of the reasons no one knew about his disorder. Or the other residual effects of captivity. He didn't need folks walking on eggshells around him.

"I'm looking for Annie," he said. "Have you heard from her?"

"Not since this morning. I had some trouble with my son and we talked a couple of times."

He hadn't realized Becky had a son. Had only just recently put together that Annie's best friend was also Luke Chisum's ex. "Is everything okay?"

"As good as can be expected when a single woman is raising a fifteen-year-old boy."

"He's pushing his boundaries, huh?"

"You could say that."

Blake had no idea why he was engaging this woman in conversation. He'd never properly met her, and yet here he was, acting as if they were old friends.

Just because she knew Annie so well? Did he have it so bad that he was latching on to his ex-wife's life? Trying to live with her vicariously, since he'd never be doing so for real?

God, he hoped not.

Still...

"By the way, I didn't get a chance to thank you for the other night."

"No problem." Her voice was warm, and it occurred to Blake that Annie's best friend didn't seem all that inclined to end this conversation, either. Did that mean he had her support?

But support in what? He had no intention of having a life with Annie.

"So, you didn't hear from Annie today?" Becky's question brought him back into focus.

"No." How much did Becky know?

"Oh."

"And she didn't call you?" Did they each know what they were talking about?

"No. But if there was a problem, she would have. She always does."

Was that supposed to be reassurance? How about if there'd been news of a baby? Or not.

Thanking Becky again, Blake rang off, frustrated, worried and just plain in a grouchy mood.

AT SIX, keys in hand, Blake dialed June Lawry. Having become reacquainted with June while visiting with Cole over the past couple of years, Blake figured she was his final hope.

"Blake, good to hear from you," the older woman said, her voice kind and welcoming.

Biding his time through the pleasantries, Blake tried to figure out, now that he had Annie's mother on the phone, how to ask about her daughter.

And in the end, he just came out with it. "You wouldn't happen to know where Annie is, would you? I've been trying to reach her and can't get her to pick up."

"Yes, as a matter of fact, I do know." June's tone was more tentative. "She's here, actually."

At her mother's? As a rule, Annie could hardly be dragged to the home she'd grown up in for an hour for Christmas dinner, let alone at any other time during the year. "She is."

"Yes. She's been here most of the afternoon."

"She has."

Had Blake not been married to this woman's daughter for several years, he might not have understood that June was telling him something. But they both knew Annie just didn't hang out at her mother's.

"Is she okay?"

"She's having kind of a hard time at the moment, but overall she's fine."

"Is she right there?"

"No, she's back in my bedroom. She fell asleep about half an hour ago."

Annie asleep? At—he checked his watch—five after six?

"Did she, uh, get some bad news today?"

"I don't think so, why?"

June knew something. She had to. But for some reason, she didn't know that Blake would be aware that today had had special significance for Annie.

"June, I know about Annie's plans," he said, still careful, on the off chance that Annie hadn't told her mother everything.

In the days of their marriage, it would have been a given. But more things had changed than he'd realized.

"You do."

"Yes."

"She told you."

"Yes."

"Oh."

"So…can you tell me what she found out today?"

The pause on the other end of the line hung heavy. "I… I'd like to, Blake, but you know Annie. She's so careful. And she came to me, you know? This is the first time in…"

"I understand." He couldn't be angry with the woman. Because he knew exactly what this day must have meant to Annie's mom.

Locking the door of his office, he strode down the hall toward the elevator, cell phone at his ear.

"If you don't mind my asking," June said, curiosity evident in her voice, "what do you have to do with this?"

Blake had already figured out that the question was coming. As soon as he'd let it be known that he knew Annie was trying to start a family.

"If she's pregnant, I'm the father."

The words sent a curious chill through him. Not altogether an unpleasant sensation.

But not a great one, either. Had he been a whole man, he'd have been overjoyed. As it was...

He held the elevator door long enough to tell Annie's mother that he was on his way over. One way or the other, he had to know what they were facing.

As the potential father of the child, he had a right to know.

June didn't try to dissuade him.

"And Blake?" she asked as he was hanging up.

"Yes, ma'am?"

"Welcome back to the family."

Afraid that he'd just triggered an avalanche that was going to have far-reaching effects, Blake nevertheless didn't have the heart at the moment to correct his ex-mother-in-law's misinterpretation.

CHAPTER SIXTEEN

"I CAN'T STAY HERE, Mom. I can't see him." Standing at her mother's back door, ready to jump on her bike, Annie gave her a big hug. "Thank you for today."

"Of course," June said, tears in her eyes as she glanced at her daughter. "I'm always here. Always."

"I know that now." Annie teared up again, too. "I'm so sorry, Mom. So, so sorry. I…"

"Shh." June's finger on Annie's lips silenced her. "I made a lot of mistakes, too, Annie. None of this was your fault. You were just a child, and I expected so much of you…."

"You did your best, Mom." Annie's heart filled with love as she realized the truth in those words. "And no one can expect any more of you than that."

"Keep that in mind, sweetie." June's words, the slightly teasing smile on her face, startled Annie. It was going to take her awhile to fully grasp that, almost overnight, her mother had regained a significant position in her life.

In her reality. Everywhere else, she'd had one all along.

Annie nodded, appreciating her mom's advice. She could only do her best. That's all she could expect of herself.

Seeing the clock on the wall behind June's head, Annie said, "I gotta go. He's going to be here soon."

"I wish you'd stay…."

"I can't. I just—"

"He told me that he's your donor, Annie."

Oh. Well. For a noncommunicative man, Blake had sure chosen an inconvenient time to get chatty.

"He has a right to know."

He did. Her mother was right. Annie just wasn't in any state to see Blake. She'd spent the afternoon crying all over her mom's shoulder. And felt as if she'd been run over by a truck.

"I have to go."

"Ride carefully."

"I will."

"You're going straight home?"

June's glance was pointed. Unable to look away, like a deer in headlights, Annie stared for several seconds. And then gave a stiff nod.

"I'll tell him where to find you."

She'd been afraid of that.

BLAKE DIDN'T KNOW WHAT TO expect when he knocked on Annie's door just before eight that evening. Was he going to be a father?

Had it all been for naught?

Would Annie want to try again?

Would he?

The fact that she hadn't called weighed heavily on him. Perhaps now that she knew he was no healthier than her father, who'd committed suicide, she'd decided he wasn't acceptable as the father of her child.

If she asked him to bow out, to have nothing to do with the baby, to not be acknowledged as his father, would he?

Could he?

When she opened her door, every preconceived thought he'd had fled.

"You're crying." Without hesitation, he opened the screen door, let himself in, taking Annie's shoulders in his hands and rubbing them as he peered into her eyes.

"What's wrong, honey? If it didn't take, that's no big deal. It just means we get to enjoy trying again."

And as he said the words, he knew they were true. If Annie wanted a child, if she still wanted him to father it, he would not say no.

Rather than comforting her, consoling her, his words made her cry harder. He wasn't good with tears. Didn't know how to make them go away.

And so he pulled her into his arms and just let her cry, holding on, with the hope that somehow he was helping.

And when her legs started to wobble, he lifted her, carrying her into the living room, where he sat with her on one of the large pillows on the floor. Leaning against a wall, he cradled her until he thought she'd fallen asleep.

"I'm scared, Blake."

She hadn't moved, and still had her head lying against his chest.

"Of what?"

"Ohhh…" The drawn-out word ended in a long sigh. "I… Everything," she finally said. "Absolutely everything."

"Why, Annie?"

"Because nothing makes sense, you know?" Her words were slightly muffled against his chest, thick with held-back tears, but he understood her completely.

"I've spent my whole life with preconceived notions of how things were, thinking that they matched society's dictates about what was acceptable. When, in truth, my notions were little more than the protective, desperate understandings of a thirteen-year-old girl."

Ah. Annie was finally waking completely up. He used to wonder if there would be a day when she'd be able to face her deepest self. Had hoped to be there when and if that time came.

And it put her leagues ahead of him, now.

"Change is always scary." He quoted from one of his pamphlets. "Even good change."

"It's not just about the change. I've had enough of that in that past six years to know that anything can become routine with the passage of time."

There was real truth to that. Even lying naked on a floor started to feel normal, if one did it long enough. If there was never anything else.

"It's more that I don't trust me."

Blake frowned at this unexpected turn in the conversation. Annie was one of the most confident people he'd ever known. So sure of herself. Always.

"I've lived so rigidly, Blake, following all of my own rules, expecting those in my life to follow them, as well."

But it wasn't a bad thing. Annie knew what she wanted and wouldn't settle for less.

"And now I find that the basis for my rules doesn't exist. I've built my entire life on quicksand."

"No, Annie, you haven't. You've lived by your heart, and the life you've built is on solid ground." A man like him, someone without that stability, could easily recognize what she had. "You've got work you love and are great at. Do you know how many people go their whole lives without that? They get up every day and go to a job because it pays the bills, not because they enjoy what they're doing. They spend more waking hours at something they don't like than anything else, and then they go home tired, do a few chores, go to bed and get up to start the whole thing over again.

"But not you, Annie. You give your whole self to your day, even to the point of riding a bike to the paper so that the mundane experience of traveling to the job becomes an additional joy to you."

"You like your job." Her voice was weaker than normal, vulnerable sounding.

"Yes, I do." And he was grateful for it—every

single day. "You also have relationships that you've cultivated day after day, year after year," he told her. "Those are the most solid foundation life has to offer."

"Becky and Cole, you mean?"

"And your mother."

"I didn't cultivate that."

"Yes, you did. You stepped up to the plate for her when she could not, Annie. You helped her keep her family together, caring for Cole and the house when she wasn't around. And even after you didn't have to ever see her again, you kept in touch, spent every holiday with her. You might not have enjoyed those things. You might have resented her for making you do them—as you saw it—but the *doing* is what mattered. You planted a seed, watered it. And while you've been busy elsewhere, it's grown and matured into something that will never die."

She pushed away from him, sat up and stared.

"What?"

"Where'd all that come from?" Her mouth was open.

Put on the spot like that, Blake drew a blank.

"Do you realize that is the longest speech you've ever made to me?" Her eyes held amazement. "Maybe the only speech?"

"I'm sorry," he said, letting go of her. "I didn't mean to lecture."

"Don't apologize! I spent all the years of our marriage yearning for you to open up and talk to me. I'd gladly hear lectures every single day, if they came from you."

Seeming to realize what she'd just said, Annie quickly shut her mouth.

But she didn't take back the words.

SHE HAD TO TELL HIM. Had to talk about it. But she just wasn't ready. Couldn't find the language. Or even land on solid thoughts.

"Everything just keeps drifting away," she said, too worn-out to find it odd that here she was, at nine o'clock at night, leaning against the chest of the ex-husband she'd said she could never be with again.

The one who wouldn't let himself be with her.

"Where yesterday I had a plan, a value system, a firm understanding of right and wrong, justice and injustice, smart living and poor choices, today I'm not sure of anything."

"Sure you are." Blake's voice was soft, reassuring, and so confident that she wished she could climb right inside him and simply hold on. "You value love," he said. "Which means you value the people you love."

Yeah. He was right about that.

"And injustice is when someone is hurt, most particularly when that someone seems the least deserving of pain."

Okay.

"Right is being kind. Thinking of others. Wrong is thinking only of your own interests at the risk of taking from or hurting other people."

Yes.

"Smart living is caring for the people you love, which includes you. Tending to them physically, emotionally and mentally."

Right.

"And poor choices are any that take you away from that."

Lying there against Blake, hearing his voice reverberate in his chest, she couldn't help wondering where this man had come from.

Not because of the things he said, but because he was *saying* them. And she told him so.

"A man tends to change some when he's stripped of everything, when he's lying on rock bottom and has no way to get up."

She'd always felt Blake was deep, had loved that sense about him, had drawn great security from knowing that there was so much to him.

"I spent four years locked away by myself, Annie. I learned to value conversation."

"You're still quiet a lot."

"I'm naturally reticent, you know that," he admitted. "I like to listen. To assess. Makes me more comfortable. But at the same time, I've grown to value the ability to express my thoughts where I think they might be useful."

"You've always done that in business."

"Yes."

"So tell me about it, Blake. Tell me about those years."

He was quiet for a while and Annie hoped he

was collecting his thoughts, determining how best to give her the information she sought.

"I can't, honey." His reply disappointed her, more now because of the changes in him.

"Maybe someday I will, but for now…"

She sat up. "It's okay, Blake, I understand."

"No, Annie, I don't think you do."

The sad tone in his voice got her attention. His gaze mirrored the tone. "It's not that I'm choosing not to tell you, exactly. It's that I know if I do, I risk another episode like the one you witnessed on Friday. Becky told you that I know the signs—that I can tell when one is coming."

Hanging on to the words he was giving her, Annie nodded.

"It's all part of something they call management," he continued. "You learn how to manage yourself, your very life, rather than simply 'live' it. Because only then can you hope to function in society."

It broke her heart to hear him say that. And yet, she knew instantly that he was telling her the truth.

"Then I'll wait," she said, vowing that there would be a day, someday, when Blake would be able to tell her everything. Just one friend talking to another.

HE HAD TO GO. Ten o'clock was rolling around, and Annie needed to get some rest. And he had a long drive back to San Antonio.

But he couldn't leave yet. Not without hearing what had happened that day. He'd pretty much figured out she wasn't pregnant. He just wasn't sure where she was going next with that part of her life.

And whether or not he was still part of the plan.

He didn't know how to broach the subject. Didn't want to upset her again.

"Talk to me, sweetie."

Her fingers curled around the edges of his shirt. "Do you think I'm wrong, Blake? To want a child, even though I have no intention of getting married?"

That's what this was all about?

"Of course not. I wouldn't have agreed to help you if I thought that. The world has changed so much since we were kids," he said. "With the Internet making the planet so much smaller, more accessible, people are moving around more, leaving very few of us with lives like you find here in River Bluff—lives where folks live in the same houses for decades, and where they end up married to their neighbor. Their kids go to the same schools they went to, and their first-grade teacher becomes the older lady sitting next to them in the church choir."

Another one of his fantasies during his time away—one of his favorites—had been to imagine growing up in such a town. Being a hometown boy, with roots that reached back generations. In those dreams, he'd even gone as far as to build and furnish the house that he'd always lived in.

And moved Annie in with him.

They'd had four kids. One child to hold with each hand.

"Women have careers now. A good many mothers aren't at home, waiting for their kids with cookies and milk, when school gets out. And with all the changes comes a higher divorce rate, too, which means more single-parent homes. It's more the norm than not, I sometimes think."

Annie hadn't moved. She finally murmured, "Becky's on the brink of having real problems with her son, and she's feeling completely ineffective. She can see that he's headed for trouble, and can't seem to do, or threaten to do, anything that will turn him around. He needs a father figure."

"I thought she lived with her dad."

"He's a retired sheriff. A real stickler. And far too strict. He always was, which is why the Wild Bunch dared Luke Chisum to ask her out, even though Hub Parker threatened to kill him if he ever caught Luke, his next-door neighbor, around his daughter."

"You think she dated Luke to get back at her father? Not because she really liked him?"

"Oh, don't get me wrong." Annie's voice was growing stronger. "Becky loved Luke with all her heart—a heart that man broke when he left town and joined the army."

There was no doubt what Annie thought of Luke's choice. But Blake wondered if she liked the man himself.

He certainly did.

"Some boys get into trouble whether they're with two parents or one, a mother *or* a father," he said. "Maybe it's something in the hormones, that drive to get out there and see for yourself. To be in control of one's own destiny, even when, in fact, he's too young to have any idea what that might be."

"Maybe," she said. "Becky's done a great job with Shane, though. She's done her best. But she didn't choose single parenthood. It was thrust upon her. Any failures aren't her fault."

Blake didn't miss the innuendo, pointing right back at herself, and he hated to hear so much self-doubt from someone who knew her own mind so well. Blake had to go, but he couldn't leave things like this.

"In the first place, if and when you do have a baby, you're going to be a great mother, Annie. Failure isn't something you need to worry about."

And—he wanted to add—*if our deal is still on, you aren't going to be doing this alone. That child will have a father figure.*

Just not one who slept with his mom.

"If and when?" Annie asked, sitting up, her hand still on his chest, almost as if she'd forgotten it was there. "Didn't Mom tell you?"

"Tell me what?"

"I'm pregnant, Blake. The test was positive."

He was going to be a daddy.

It was Blake's turn to have eyes filled with tears.

"WE HAVE TO DISCUSS logistics," Annie said just before eleven that night. She'd changed, since she'd found out he hadn't known about the baby. Grown more distant.

And less vulnerable.

Suspecting her show of strength was mostly an act to convince herself, Blake nonetheless let it stand at face value.

He'd been thinking a lot about the *practical* reality of sharing a child with his ex-wife. And had, several times, come to the same conclusion. He knew it was the right decision. Now to convince Annie of that.

"I need to know what you expect in terms of shared parenting," she said. "We really should have ironed all of this out before we ever…"

He wondered what thought she hadn't completed. Before they had sex? Or before they made love.

"I've been thinking about that," he told her, wondering how best to approach her with his plan. How to present it without giving her the wrong idea. "Did you mean it when you said you never intend to marry again?"

"Completely. I've had the love of my life, and I've had security, and neither worked. I can't take the chance on having my heart broken a third time. I can't trust that a marriage would ever work."

"You're sure about that?"

"As sure as I am that I want this baby."

In the end, he probably didn't do the plan justice.

"Then I think we should get married."

Annie's silence wasn't what he'd wanted. She'd

been sitting on a pillow beside him, leaning against the wall a couple of inches away. Feet out in front of her, she seemed inordinately interested in her toes.

"Not to live together," he quickly assured her. "We both know that wouldn't work. And frankly, for reasons you now understand, I can't risk it. But you have to admit, there are a lot of practical advantages to the legal aspects of the arrangement."

As far as proposals went, this had to be the all-time worst. But then, he wasn't proposing a romantic union.

"Such as?"

At least she hadn't immediately said no. Hadn't jumped up and kicked him out on his butt. Could it be that she was actually considering his idea?

Blake hardly dared hope. Gathering his thoughts, he set out to present the most important business proposition of his life.

"Insurance, for one thing," he said. "I don't know what your benefits at the paper are, but considering its small size, I'm guessing if you have full coverage, it's expensive."

"It is."

"I have an interest in more than one insurance company, which nets me the best health-care coverage available at a nominal rate. The rate extends to my immediate family."

In today's world of rising health-care costs and disbanding insurance companies, this was probably his strongest selling point.

"Second, if something were to happen to me,

you and the baby would be taken care of for the rest of your lives. Everything I have would automatically be yours. And if something happened to *you*, the baby would still be mine. We wouldn't have to worry about court intervention.

"Marriage between us would also make things such as school enrollment and even doctor visits that much easier. We'd both have the right to represent the child.

"We would all have the same last name, too, which would make things less confusing." He was scraping the bottom of the barrel now, but she still wasn't talking. Wasn't giving him any indication at all what she was thinking.

"There'd be no sex?"

He'd do his best on that one. But... "If that's the way you want it." He'd never take Annie against her will.

He just wasn't so sure that was how it would work out. Their record for keeping their hands off each other wasn't exactly stellar.

"And you're still going to live in San Antonio?"

"My business is there."

"Mine's here."

"I know."

"How would we explain it to everyone?"

"Tell them to mind their own business. How is this any worse than you having a baby on your own?"

"I'd still have the final say in this child's life," she said, and Blake's heart sped up.

She was seriously considering this.

He'd never actually thought she would.

"Agreed."

"Do you plan to be involved even before the baby's born?"

He hadn't allowed himself to think that far, but… "Yes."

"Doctor's visits, too?"

"Yes."

She glanced at him a time or two. "And no sex."

"If that's the way you want it."

He could hardly breathe. But the tightness in his chest was panic-based. He felt a rebirth of hope combined with good old-fashioned excitement.

"Okay, then I'll marry you." Annie's words were every dream he'd had in that hellhole come true.

"But no sex."

CHAPTER SEVENTEEN

ONCE HE HAD HER AGREEMENT to marry, Blake wanted to get it done as quickly as possible. The baby was already coming, and he wanted everything securely tied up before the first doctor's appointment.

He wanted to attend that visit as the baby's legal father, as Annie's next of kin and as the one who would have power of attorney if anything ever happened to her.

Annie hoped that, deep inside, in those places Blake didn't dare access, he just really wanted to marry her again that badly.

And she feared the same. Going in with her eyes open this time meant that she knew there were no guarantees in life. No harbor that was completely safe. Life didn't work that way.

Losing her little-girl perspective was hard. But liberating, at the same time. The world was a new place, full of possibility, now that the constraints of unrealistic expectation didn't hold her back.

It was also fraught with the pitfalls that she'd pretended to herself, all these years, she'd been avoiding.

"Are you sure this is what you want to do?" Becky asked her Wednesday evening as they shared a salad at the local restaurant while Becky waited for Shane to finish football practice. She, or her father, were taking him to and from every single activity, including school, for the next several weeks.

She'd nailed his window shut. And had spent the previous evening scrubbing at his door hinge until it had a permanent squeak.

"I'm sure," Annie told her friend, her mind coming back to Becky's question. And she was. Scared, but completely sure.

"So what's changed? Why is it you think he's not going to break your heart again?"

"He might," Annie said simply. "But my heart's not any better off without him than it would be if I'm with him and he breaks it. I hurt either way. I guess I'd rather hurt with him than without him."

"So be friends with him. It doesn't mean you have to marry him."

Frowning, Annie asked, "You don't think I should? You think the PTSD makes him a bad prospect? Too high a risk?"

Didn't really matter at this point—Annie was committed. But Eyes Open being her new motto, she wanted to know.

"Absolutely not." Becky's adamant reply left no doubt about that. "And I'm not against you marrying him, though I'd be happier for you if it were more than just a legal agreement. Mostly, I want to make certain that you know *why* you're doing it."

Leave it to Becky to force the hard issues, to pull things from Annie that she didn't want to look at. She could always count on her for that.

And valued her for it, too. Most of the time.

This wasn't one of those times.

"It makes sense," she said now, forking up a piece of lettuce with more force than was probably necessary.

"Annie?"

She glanced up into Becky's concerned eyes. "You don't marry for the sake of 'sense.'"

"It's not a real marriage."

"So, Blake didn't stay with you last night?"

"Of course not. You know he can't sleep anywhere but his home."

"I know no such thing. Of course he can. He travels, doesn't he?"

Becky had her there. But… "Where he's in hotel rooms by himself."

"So tell me you didn't make love last night before he left."

That was really none of Becky's business. Except that Annie had given her friend the right to be that much into her life a long time ago.

Her lack of a reply was all the response Becky needed.

"You love him, Annie. Not only that, you're still *in love* with him. Just admit it."

That wasn't something she wanted to do.

But eventually, with a fresh flood of tears, she did.

COLE LEANED OVER AFTER Blake's second loss. "You okay?" he asked, low enough for only Blake to hear.

"Fine." He grinned at his friend. "Just not concentrating."

Luke dealt the next hand and Blake tipped the corners of his cards, then tossed them into the middle of the table. Cole did the same.

"Any particular reason you aren't concentrating?"

Blake shrugged, pretending to watch the game, while watching his soon-to-be brother-in-law out of the corner of his eye. A surge of affection, of gratitude, swept through him—a sensation more natural and comfortable than any he'd felt, aside from what he'd experienced being with Annie, since his return.

Having Cole know about his challenges wasn't as bad as he'd thought it would be. Instead of feeling trapped, marked, Blake found a curious kind of strength in Cole's concern and support.

As if he didn't have to bear the entire brunt of his situation alone. It was good to know someone was watching out for him. Even if that someone was a worrywart. And had become more of an irritating parent than the guy friend he was used to.

The hand folded and Hap stood to get another beer. They were still playing in the back room of the Wild Card Saloon, waiting to hear from Jake, but they knew it might be their last time together in the old bar. Blake hadn't played with the group anywhere else.

Brady, sitting two down from Blake, shuffled the cards. "You heading to the Henley farms?" Blake asked, as four of the eight men sitting there left the table, either to get more to eat or use the facilities.

"Don't know yet." Brady's face was tight as he continued to shuffle. "Can't get the old man to commit one way or the other. My guess is he's checking up on the lead himself. I appreciate the tip, though, Blake. I've been on the hunt for months, and this horse your guy found is by far the best out there. He's exactly what I want. If I had the means, I'd just go buy the damn thing myself, and show my father what I can do."

"He seems like a fair man," Blake said.

"He is. I don't blame him for not trusting me with this. It was stupid of me to run off to Las Vegas and gamble my fortune away after the Cowboys let me go. My father's skepticism is only part of the price I'm paying for that foolhardiness."

"I have an idea you aren't going to be paying all that much longer," Blake said, eyeing the older man who, with Luke, was uncapping another beer. Tonight's game was the first time Marshall Carrick had joined them. He'd played in the old days, but since Brady's return, the general understanding had been that Marshall refused to join the game as a way of showing him he wasn't going to support the thing that had been his son's downfall.

Brady's gaze followed Blake's and, still tight-lipped, he nodded. "Maybe."

"He's here," Blake pointed out.

"Probably to check up on me."

"Or to see that you really are playing a mature—and cheap—game of poker with friends," Blake finished quietly, as the others started filtering back to the table. He was feeling generous about the world tonight. Life might not be turning out as he'd envisioned some years ago, but it was a hell of a lot better than he'd dared hope during the past two years.

Annie in his life, in any capacity, was a gift.

"There's that grin again," Cole said, as Ron Hayward took his seat at Blake's left, giving Harry Knutson a heads-up that he felt a win coming on. With a couple of good hands under his belt, the cocky man was just getting cockier.

Blake was glad to know him.

"I asked Annie to marry me," Blake finally said under his breath, knowing that Cole knew damn well why he was feeling so good. Annie had called that afternoon to let him know that she'd told her mother, Cole and Becky that they were getting married.

Blake had told Colin and Marta, too, leaving out the part about the baby for now. Marta had started to cry, and Colin shook his hand for a solid minute.

"Hey, everybody! Did you hear that?" Cole jumped up before Brady could get the cards around the table. "Blake just said he's getting married!"

Blake understood, then, that Cole had just been waiting for an opportunity to announce the news.

The ruckus that broke out almost had him running for his car. The river. Anyplace but that small, noisy room. Except that he was too darn busy deflecting the good-natured razzing to even think about getting away.

"When's the wedding?" Harry asked, and Blake remembered what Cole had told him about the older man. Once you told Harry something, he told his hairdresser wife, and it would be all around town in the morning.

"We don't know yet," he said. "Soon, though."

"Hey." Luke grinned, tipping a bottle of beer to his lips. "We should all go to Vegas this weekend. Not only are the cards good, but they do weddings every hour on the hour. It's all legal and quick."

"Imagine the Wild Bunch loose on the strip," Brady said with a noticeable dryness.

"It's not a bad idea," Cole piped up, and Blake, seeing the hesitant look on Brady's face, wondered if they weren't all being a bit insensitive. The last time Brady had played cards in Vegas, a man had committed suicide.

Marshall Carrick wasn't saying much, just playing with his chips.

"I say let's do it," Luke declared. "Brady needs to go back, to face his demons, and what better way to do that than with all of us there together for a happy occasion?"

"I don't know." Brady finished the deal.

"I think you should go," Harry said. "Even if there isn't a wedding."

Blake threw in his cards. Shuffling his chips, Cole did not. Luke pulled his hat down.

And the challenge had been issued.

"I agree with Harry, son." Marshall's quiet words filled the room and everyone froze. "You need to go back, show yourself what you're made of. And if you do, if you come home, we'll go to that sale."

And just like that, it was settled. Blake was going to Vegas over the weekend to get married.

Assuming the bride agreed to the plan.

"YOU READY FOR THIS?" Becky fluffed the curls that fell most of the way down Annie's back in their room at the Mirage Saturday afternoon. The two of them had arrived the night before and, other than having a long visit from June, who was just down the hall, along with Cole, they'd seen no one.

They'd slept. Ordered room service.

And talked for most of the night.

Becky was there for Annie. She wanted nothing to do with Luke.

"Completely ready," Annie said. She was nervous, afraid of some of the challenges that lay ahead, of not having a clear, controlled plan for the protection of her heart, but adamantly certain she was doing the right thing. The best thing.

For her, the only thing. She belonged with Blake.

Just as June had belonged with Tim Lawry. For better or worse.

"You know, I watched my mom run her hands over the wood on my cradle. And as she talked, I could remember my father doing the same sort of thing. He was gifted, Bec. That man could look at wood and see amazing things."

"I know, honey."

"He had weaknesses, but we all do."

"Yes."

"I let my memory of the bad overshadow the good."

"You were a kid, Ann, with the responsibility of an adult suddenly thrust upon you. You did what you could."

"I had my own weaknesses," Annie said, looking at herself in the mirror. The wide blue eyes, a child's eyes, finally seeing the world from an adult perspective. "I hurt my mother so much."

"You both got hurt."

"But the thing is, she's always loved me. Even now, all it took was for me to go to her, and there were no recriminations or blame. No judgments. Just love."

Becky smiled, nodded.

"She loved my father that same way."

"That's what love is, honey. It allows us to see the good, in spite of the bad. And if it's working right, it gives us the strength to cope with the not-so-good."

"That's where I got messed up," she said. "I somehow got it in my head that it was up to me to choose people in my life who wouldn't hurt me. When, instead, I was hurting myself because by those standards, I haven't let anyone love me."

The concept was convoluted. Not at all black-and-white, easily defined or understood. It wasn't rigid. But it was life.

If she was ever going to be happy, she had to understand that everyone had weaknesses, to forgive them any pain they caused, and allow herself to love, to accept love, in spite of everything.

Annie was ready to do that. To start living for real.

GLANCING AT HIS WATCH, Blake took a long, deep breath. This was it. The next few hours would bring so much change.

"You ready?" Cole asked. They were due downstairs in ten minutes.

"Not just yet," he replied, listening for a knock on the door. It had to come. Now was the time.

He'd made some phone calls. Pulled some strings with one of the government agents who'd worked closely with him after his release.

He was due to testify at the trial of his captors in another six months or so.

And he knew now that when he did so, he'd have the backing and support of an entire family of friends. Annie and Cole. But the Wild Bunch, too.

It was time they were all together again.

All of them.

"We gotta go, man," said Cole, looking impressive in his black suit as he glanced at his watch for about the tenth time in as many minutes. "Probably wouldn't be a good idea to keep Annie waiting."

Annie wasn't expecting him just yet.

"You afraid she's going to run out on me?" Blake asked, loosening his tie. He always could retie the knot. Buy himself a few more minutes.

"This is Annie we're talking about," Cole said. "I can't believe she agreed to marry you at all. Let's get this done before she comes up with some other harebrained scheme that she'll fight to the death to bring about."

The knot was tied. His shirt tucked in. Belt latched. Shoes shined...

And there was a rap on the door.

"You want to get that?" he asked Cole, pretending to check the contents of his pocket, while keeping an eye on the scene unfolding before him.

"It's probably Mom, telling us that Annie's getting antsy." Cole pulled open the door as he spoke, and then just stopped and stared.

"Jake?"

"I heard there was a Wild Bunch wedding going on." The six-foot-tall, thin but muscular man stood at the door, a cocky grin on his lips, and something a bit deeper in his dark eyes, as he stared at Cole.

"Jake Chandler. I don't believe it." Cole just stood there, staring. "Wow."

"Might want to let him in, Cole," Blake said, sweating a bit as he came forward.

"Yeah, seems like I should meet the groom, if I'm going to be standing up at his wedding with the rest of the bunch." Jake's slow, easy walk as he stepped into the room, his longish hair, made it easy to believe the devil-may-care stories Blake had heard about him.

"Jake. Damn. I can't believe it's you." Cole reached out to shake the other man's hand, and then pulled him into a back-pounding hug.

Blake had done good.

Jake was home.

"LADIES AND GENTLEMEN. We are gathered here today to witness the marriage of Annie Marie Kincaid to Blake Edward Smith…."

Trembling, Annie stood in the garish red room, surrounded by velvet draperies and images of Elvis, enough flowers to make her slightly dizzy and music that was too loud. But with all of her loved ones around her, she knew that she was in the middle of a perfect moment.

As she gave her hand to Blake, she had a fleeting thought of her father, as if he were smiling down at her, giving his blessing to the union.

Giving Annie away to the man she loved with all her heart.

With Becky and her mom standing on one side of them, and Luke, Jake, Cole and Brady—the Wild Bunch complete—on the other, she listened to the man who was officiating as he spoke about sacred duties, compromise and understanding. Having expected a quick, generic ceremony, considering their surroundings, and not really caring as long as she was married to Blake when they were done, Annie was impressed with the man's offering.

Blake stood beside her, steady, seemingly calm. Holding her hand as if he'd never let it go.

There was a brief second of sadness when she glanced over to catch Luke Chisum staring at Becky Howard—with a longing in his eyes that Annie understood.

She knew that feeling. She was marrying Blake, but he wasn't hers yet. And she needed him to be. More than anything else, she needed him sharing every aspect of her life, living with her, loving her.

Fully married to her in the eyes of God, the world, and in her eyes, too.

Did Luke still love Becky that way? Hard to believe, considering all the time that had passed. And yet, considering the force that had pulled Annie and Blake together in this place, in spite of all the history between and around them, it wasn't hard to believe at all.

Somehow, some way, she had to get Becky to release the fear in her heart enough to talk to Luke. To at least see.

Becky deserved a chance at real happiness. Especially now, with Shane giving her such challenges. She'd gone it alone long enough.

"Do you, Blake Edward Smith, take this woman to be your lawfully wedded wife, in sickness and in health, until death you do part?"

"I do."

"Do you, Annie Marie Kincaid, take this man to be your lawfully wedded husband, in sickness and in health, until death you do part?"

"I do."

"Please turn and face each other."

Doing as she was told, Annie thought about the ring she'd slipped to Becky. The one she'd given Blake more than ten years before. The one he'd handed to her for safekeeping when he'd left on that business trip to the Middle East six years ago.

Blake, with a searching look, took both of her hands in his, and Annie knew, in that second, that they were going to be okay. Really okay.

Blake Smith didn't know what had hit him yet. But he would. Just as soon as they got off the plane in San Antonio that night.

She held out her left hand when instructed, and couldn't stop the tears from springing to her eyes as she felt the thin gold band slide onto her finger. And then, turning to Becky, she took her own offering, holding Blake's gaze as she slid his wedding ring back where it belonged.

She wasn't sure he recognized it. Didn't expect he would. And then she felt his hand tremble in hers. Saw the moisture in his eyes and knew that he had.

"Don't you ever take this off again," she said, interrupting the ceremony in a loud and clear voice. Her own wedding poem.

"Never." It was that vow that Annie heard, over and over, as their group went up to a penthouse dinner and then, changing clothes, took the limousine Blake had arranged back to the airport.

There was to be no gambling today. They would

form a circle around Brady Carrick and get him safely home.

Because that's what they did. Formed circles of love around each other and shared strengths where there were weaknesses.

THE PLANE LANDED, they claimed their baggage and, after a quick exchange with Cole, June and Becky, Annie stepped alongside Blake. He saw the exchange. Didn't know what it meant.

Jake Chandler had come back to Texas with them, intending to arrange a funeral for his uncle, deal with the bar and then head back to California. But he was going to stay in touch this time.

This was where the party ended for the day. Annie had her car. Blake had his. She had her home in River Bluff. His was in San Antonio.

And he was okay with that. Fate had seen fit to give him this second chance to have Annie as a part of his life. And he would not waste a single moment mourning for what might have been. For what couldn't be. He would, instead, be grateful every day of his life.

Luke and Brady had driven together and, calling out their farewells, they headed off before the rest of them. Blake didn't mean to interrupt, to observe something that was absolutely none of his business, but he couldn't help noticing the long glance Luke Chisum gave Becky Howard as he took his leave.

As far as Blake knew, the two had never exchanged so much as a word during the entire twenty-four hours they'd been in Las Vegas.

Clearly, they should have. There was something to be said between them. That much was obvious.

And maybe it was his business. Just as his business was theirs. Something to talk to Annie about.

Sometime. Over the phone. Or in the waiting room at the doctor's office.

The members of their group slowly peeled off, going to their cars. Cole and his mother drove away, and that left only Blake's wife and her best friend. The two women had driven to San Antonio together. Which meant that Blake wouldn't have a moment alone with Annie before they parted.

But he could call her later. Thank her for marrying him. Tell her that he was glad they'd done what they had that day. That he had no regrets.

"Okay, call me." Becky's words reached him. The women were leaving. But why would Becky want him to call her? "See ya, Blake." She walked to her car and got in.

Leaving Annie standing there.

"Let's go," she said brusquely, moving past him, wheeling her bag behind her.

"Where are you going?"

"To your car."

Standing there perplexed, and then maybe a bit frustrated, angry or something, Blake called out to her. "It's not over there."

Annie turned around, came back, passed him and continued on her way.

"It's not there, either."

"Then where the hell is it?" she asked, standing before him.

"Annie, what are you doing?"

"Going home with my husband." Her chin was lifted, her eyes daring him to argue with her.

"Don't do this, Annie. Don't make it any harder than it already is."

"No, Blake, you have that wrong. I'm not the one making this hard. You are. You, with your antiquated thoughts of a man always having to be the strong one. Open your mind a bit, would you? The world has changed. Life has changed. We have changed. Now are you going to tell me where the car is or not?"

Four different parties had stopped to look at them in the garage, as they passed on the way to their vehicles.

That was the only reason Blake led Annie toward the Continental, unlocked the trunk and went to lift her bag inside beside his own.

"I can get it," she said, hauling the thing up with one hand and easily depositing it in the trunk.

She moved to the passenger door. Instinctively going to open it for her, Blake stopped. Annie was trying to make some kind of point, and he knew her well enough to know that she'd make it one way or another, sooner or later. He'd just as soon have it be sooner, so he could get her out of his car and safely back to River Bluff.

Climbing in beside her, he put the key in the ignition but didn't start the car.

"What's going on, Annie?"

"We are, Blake," she said, half mimicking him. But her gaze had softened, with compassion, vulnerability, and also a knowing determination that he didn't think he'd ever seen there before.

"My father committed suicide," she said bluntly, reminding him of another thing he loved about Annie. She was always surprising him.

"I know."

"It wasn't his fault."

"I believe that."

"I didn't. Not for a long time. He was a good man, Blake. He lived a good life. Created beautiful things, not only with his hands, but with his love. He made our family."

"Of course he did."

"He cared for us as long as he could, and when he couldn't anymore, we cared for ourselves, because that's what families do. They take up the slack for the people they love."

Blake could see where she was going with this. And couldn't let her do it.

"I love you, Blake Smith. More than life. More than anything I can think of. I'm not complete without you. And I'd rather live my life mad at you sometimes, frustrated with you, but always loving you, than be alone without the risk of ever having you hurt me again."

"I can't, Annie." His heart almost burst with what it took him to say that. "I just can't."

"You don't trust me."

"I don't trust *me*."

"Well, I do. And that'll just have to be enough for both of us."

He had to make her see.

"I mean it, Blake. I'm not getting out of this car until you take me to your home, where I would like to be carried over the threshold. And then I need some loving. Lots and lots of it. Hours of it. Until you're so exhausted you can't possibly climb out of our bed, and you fall asleep in my arms instead."

"I have a night stalker." He'd never have believed he'd say the words, if he hadn't just clearly heard them.

"A cat that comes around?" Annie asked, frowning.

"No. A demon that opens my bedroom door at night and jumps on my chest."

"Okay." She didn't even flinch. "Does he have a name?"

"No." She wasn't taking this seriously. And, really, that was for the best. He'd laugh it off. Take her home to River Bluff and make her get out of his car.

"Does he visit every night?"

"No."

"How often does he come?"

"I don't know," Blake said, running a hand through his hair, feeling exhausted all of a sudden. "A few times a year. Unless I'm under a lot of stress."

"Has he been by a lot lately?"

"Once. A couple of weeks ago."

"I'd say you've been under a hell of a lot of stress, lately," she said.

"For me, yes."

"And he only came once?"

"What's your point, Annie?"

"I'm not afraid of him, Blake. I'm not afraid of any of your demons. I'm stronger than they are. I want to be the light in your darkness."

With a soft grasp, she took hold of his chin, leaned forward until they were almost nose to nose, and looked him straight in the eye.

"Listen to me carefully, Blake," she said succinctly. "I am not afraid of you."

And with six innocuous little words, Annie freed him from the hell that he'd believed eternal.

"We'll watch the warning signs, love," she said, wiping a tear from his cheek. "You'll teach me, and we'll watch them together. And if we miss some, if there's an episode, I'll avoid your punch. Okay? I'll always avoid your punch."

He didn't know what to say. Now, at the most critical time, he couldn't find words.

"Just say okay."

"Okay." And then, as though the one word released a dam, he couldn't stop. "Oh, God, Annie, what you do to me. You have always been the sunshine in my heart, do you know that? I'd rather die than lose that again."

"You are everything to me, Blake. You always have been. Which is why we need each other so badly."

She was right. He could see that now.

"You have to promise me that you'll keep yourself safe, when I can't do it for you," he said now, completely firm. Without that promise he'd walk away. "No heroics, Annie."

"No heroics, I promise."

"I mean it."

"I loaded my own suitcase, Blake. I can always do that as long as you're there beside me opening the trunk. And I can open the trunk, too, if you need me to."

He couldn't believe this was happening. That the skies had finally opened, giving him back his life. And giving his life to her.

"Don't ever let me shut you out," he said now drawing her forehead to his with a hand behind her neck. "Push me, nag me, yell at me, if that's what it takes, but keep with me until the words come. Because I want them to, Annie. I had too many years of needing to talk to you and having you not be there. I don't ever want that to happen again."

"I know," she said, wetting her lips as she smiled. "And I know, now, that your quietness is just you, not a reflection of your feelings for me. I'm okay with that. I actually kind of like it. Someone like Cole would drive me crazy—"

That last word got lost as Blake covered her mouth with his own.

He'd been gone a long time. Taken against his will, held captive while he fought with everything he had to free himself. Fought to endure. To hang on. To rise above. To survive. It seemed like he'd been fighting his way out forever.

And right there, in the front seat of an old Lincoln Continental, in the parking garage of the San Antonio airport, Blake Smith finally won.

* * * * *

*Don't miss the Wild Bunch heroes
when they deal out their Texas Hold'em hands
again next month—and really up the ante!
Look for Cole's story,
BETTING ON SANTA (SR #1452)
by Debra Salonen in November 2007,
wherever Harlequin books are sold.
Turn the page for a sneak peek....*

"CAREFUL. CAREFUL. We gotta turn it sideways. Trust me. It won't fit head-on."

"We know, Ron. That's why I suggested taking it through the patio door," Cole's pal Brady Carrick said.

"This door's wider. I built the place. I should know," Ron argued.

Brady, who was on the same end of the table as Cole, smirked. Cole knew Ron wasn't one of Brady's favorite alternate poker players, but Brady wasn't the type to make a scene. He got things done his way and didn't make a big deal about it. Unlike Ron, who went out of his way to call the shots.

But since Cole was holding up one corner of the beastly heavy table that Ron had donated so Cole could host the upcoming poker game, he kept his criticism to himself.

"Holy heck, this thing weighs a ton, Ron. What's it made of—brick?" Luke Chisum, another of Cole's poker buddies, asked.

"If it was brick it wouldn't get scratched," a female voice quipped.

"You're a big help, Annie," Cole said, using his shoulder to brace the table. His ankle was already starting to throb and he was carrying only one fifth of the weight. "Could you at least keep the door open?"

"Cole, where do you want this damn thing?" Blake asked, his voice gruff with exertion. "You know I *pay* people to do this kind of thing, don't you?"

"Suck it up, man. Those biceps are going to waste away from counting beans all day," Brady challenged.

"A lot of beans," Luke added. "Did you see the car he's driving?"

"That's Annie's car," Blake countered.

"Which she refuses to drive because it isn't a bio-diesel," Annie said from beside the door she was holding open. "I told him, 'Global warming,' and he said, 'Heated seats.' The conversation went downhill from there."

Cole snickered. His sister was too much at times, but he loved it that she stuck by her principles.

"I said, 'Side airbags and highest safety rating of all SUVs in its class,'" Blake countered. "It's a whole heck of a lot safer than a bike seat and a helmet."

"I've heard you can buy those pull-along baby carriers with titanium roll bars," Luke said. Luke was their resident jokester.

"Really?" Annie asked, sounding interested.

Blake groaned. "Don't encourage her."

Annie, who had dashed around them once they cleared the front door, appeared at Cole's side. "Who else is coming? These are your only friends. Except for Jake, but he's still hiding out at the Card."

"I have tons of friends. They just don't live around here."

"The people you're referring to in San Antonio aren't your friends, Cole. They were work associates, and most of them erased your name from their Palm Pilots the minute Big Jim told them you were persona non grata. Those aren't friends."

She was right, which pissed him off.

"These guys might be losers, but at least they're real," his sister added.

"Losers?" Brady sputtered. "I played for the Dallas Cowboys."

"I have a purple heart," Luke called out.

"Jake's a millionaire," Blake interjected.

Annie put her hands on her hips. "I meant that in a tough-love, big-sister-to-you-all kind of way. You're not loser losers, but you are in your thirties and living back at home, and none of you are married or have any children."

"Mine is on the way, and Cole might already be a daddy," Blake said as they carefully muscled the table into an upright position and lowered it to its legs.

Every person in the room looked at Blake. It took the man a moment to realize what he'd just said, then he shook his head and swore. "I can't believe I did that. Annie, this is your fault. You know how much I like to win an argument. Sorry, Cole."

The place erupted, with everyone speaking at once.

Cole blew out a sigh. He'd known the saga would come out eventually.

* * * * *

Silhouette® Romantic Suspense
keeps getting hotter!
Turn the page for a sneak preview of
Wendy Rosnau's latest SPY GAMES *title*
SLEEPING WITH DANGER

Available November 2007

Silhouette® Romantic Suspense—
Sparked by Danger, Fueled by Passion!

Melita had been expecting a chaste quick kiss of the generic variety. But this kiss with Sully was the kind that sparked a dying flame to life. The kind of kiss you can't plan for. The kind of kiss memories are built on.

The memory of her murdered lover, Nemo, came to her then and she made a starved little noise in the back of her throat. She raised her arms and threaded her fingers through Sully's hair, pulled him closer. Felt his body settle, then melt into her.

In that instant her hunger for him grew, and his for her. She pressed herself to him with more urgency, and he responded in kind.

Melita came out of her kiss-induced memory of

Nemo with a start. "Wait a minute." She pushed Sully away from her. "You bastard!"

She spit two nasty words at him in Greek, then wiped his kiss from her lips.

"I thought you deserved some solid proof that I'm still in one piece." He started for the door. "The clock's ticking, honey. Come on, let's get out of here."

"That's it? You sucker me into kissing you, and that's all you have to say?"

"I'm sorry. How's that?"

He didn't sound sorry in the least. "You're—"

"Getting out of this godforsaken prison cell. Stop whining and let's go."

"Not if I was being shot at sunrise. Go. You deserve whatever you get if you walk out that door."

He turned back. "Freedom is what I'm going to get."

"A second of freedom before the guards in the hall shoot you." She jammed her hands on her hips. "And to think I was worried about you."

"If you're staying behind, it's no skin off my ass."

"Wait! What about our deal?"

"You just said you're not coming. Make up your mind."

"Have you forgotten we need a boat?"

"How could I? You keep harping on it."

"I'm not going without a boat. And those guards out there aren't going to just let you walk out of here. You need me and we need a plan."

"I already have a plan. I'm getting out of here. That's the plan."

"I should have realized that you never intended to take me with you from the very beginning. You're a liar and a coward."

Of everything she had read, there was nothing in Sully Paxton's file that hinted he was a coward, but it was the one word that seemed to register in that one-track mind of his. The look he nailed her with a second later was pure venom.

He came at her so quickly she didn't have time to get out of his way. "You know I'm not a coward."

"Prove it. Give me until dawn. I need one more night to put everything in place before we leave the island."

"You're asking me to stay in this cell one more night...and trust you?"

"Yes."

He snorted. "Yesterday you knew they were planning to harm me, but instead of doing something about it you went to bed and never gave me a second thought. Suppose tonight you do the same. By tomorrow I might damn well be in my grave."

"Okay, I screwed up. I won't do it again." Melita sucked in a ragged breath. "I can't leave this minute. Dawn, Sully. Wait until dawn." When he looked as if he was about to say no, she pleaded, "Please wait for me."

"You're asking a lot. The door's open now. I would be a fool to hang around here and trust that you'll be back."

"What you can trust is that I want off this island as badly as you do, and you're my only hope."

"I must be crazy."

"Is that a yes?"

"Dammit!" He turned his back on her. Swore twice more.

"You won't be sorry."

He turned around. "I already am. How about we seal this new deal?"

He was staring at her lips. Suddenly Melita knew what he expected. "We already sealed it."

"One more. You enjoyed it. Admit it."

"I enjoyed it because I was kissing someone else."

He laughed. "That's a good one."

"It's true. It might have been your lips, but it wasn't you I was kissing."

"If that's your excuse for wanting to kiss me, then—"

"I was kissing Nemo."

"What's a nemo?"

Melita gave Sully a look that clearly told him that he was trespassing on sacred ground. She was about to enforce it with a warning when a voice in the hall jerked them both to attention.

She bolted away from the wall. "Get back in bed. Hurry. I'll be here before dawn."

She didn't reach the door before he snagged her arm, pulled her up against him and planted a kiss on her lips that took her completely by surprise.

When he released her, he said, "If you're confused about who just kissed you, the name's Sully. I'll be here waiting at dawn. Don't be late."

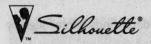

Romantic
SUSPENSE

**Sparked by Danger,
Fueled by Passion.**

Onyxx agent Sully Paxton's only chance of
survival lies in the hands of his enemy's daughter
Melita Krizova. He doesn't know he's a pawn in the
beautiful island girl's own plan for escape. Can
they survive their ruses and their fiery attraction?

**Look for the next installment in the
Spy Games miniseries,**

Sleeping with
Danger
by Wendy Rosnau

Available November 2007 wherever you buy books.

At forty, Maureen Hart suddenly finds herself juggling men. Man #1: her six-year-old grandson, left with her while his mother goes off to compete for a million dollars on reality TV. Maureen is delighted, but to Man #2— her fiancé—the little boy represents an intrusion on their time. Then Man #3, the boy's paternal grandfather, offers to take the child off her hands… and maybe even sweep Maureen off her feet….

Look for

I'M YOUR MAN

by

SUSAN CROSBY

Available November wherever you buy books.

REQUEST YOUR FREE BOOKS!
2 FREE NOVELS PLUS 2 FREE GIFTS!

HARLEQUIN®

Super Romance®

Exciting, emotional, unexpected!

YES! Please send me 2 FREE Harlequin Superromance® novels and my 2 FREE gifts. After receiving them, if I don't wish to receive any more books, I can return the shipping statement marked "cancel." If I don't cancel, I will receive 6 brand-new novels every month and be billed just $4.69 per book in the U.S., or $5.24 per book in Canada, plus 25¢ shipping and handling per book and applicable taxes, if any*. That's a savings of close to 15% off the cover price! I understand that accepting the 2 free books and gifts places me under no obligation to buy anything. I can always return a shipment and cancel at any time. Even if I never buy another book from Harlequin, the two free books and gifts are mine to keep forever.   135 HDN EEX7   336 HDN EEYK

Name	(PLEASE PRINT)	
Address		Apt.
City	State/Prov.	Zip/Postal Code

Signature (if under 18, a parent or guardian must sign)

Mail to the Harlequin Reader Service®:
IN U.S.A.: P.O. Box 1867, Buffalo, NY 14240-1867
IN CANADA: P.O. Box 609, Fort Erie, Ontario L2A 5X3

Not valid to current Harlequin Superromance subscribers.

Want to try two free books from another line?
Call 1-800-873-8635 or visit www.morefreebooks.com.

* Terms and prices subject to change without notice. NY residents add applicable sales tax. Canadian residents will be charged applicable provincial taxes and GST. This offer is limited to one order per household. All orders subject to approval. Credit or debit balances in a customer's account(s) may be offset by any other outstanding balance owed by or to the customer. Please allow 4 to 6 weeks for delivery.

Your Privacy: Harlequin is committed to protecting your privacy. Our Privacy Policy is available online at www.eHarlequin.com or upon request from the Reader Service. From time to time we make our lists of customers available to reputable firms who may have a product or service of interest to you. If you would prefer we not share your name and address, please check here. ☐

HSR07

HARLEQUIN® Romance®

New York Times bestselling author

DIANA PALMER

Handsome, eligible ranch owner Stuart York knew
Ivy Conley was too young for him, so he closed his heart
to her and sent her away—despite the fireworks between
them. Now, years later, Ivy is determined not to be
treated like a little girl anymore…but for some reason,
Stuart is always fighting her battles for her. And safe in
Stuart's arms makes Ivy feel like a woman…his woman.

Winter Roses

Available November.

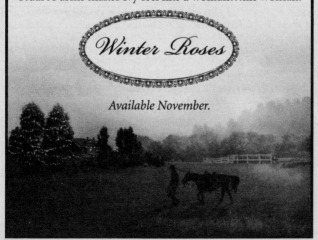

COMING NEXT MONTH

#1452 BETTING ON SANTA • Debra Salonen
Texas Hold 'Em

When Tessa Jamison sets out to find the father of her sister's toddler, she doesn't expect to like anything about Cole Lawry, a carpenter with humble aspirations. Theirs is a secret-baby story with a twist. Because when it comes to love, the stakes are high....

#1453 A CHRISTMAS TO REMEMBER • Kay Stockham

A soldier wakes up in a hospital unable to remember anything. Before he can regain his memory, he runs into the woman he once betrayed. He can't believe that he could ever do anything to hurt someone, but there's no other explanation. Or is there?

#1454 SNOWBOUND • Janice Kay Johnson

Fiona MacPherson takes refuge from a raging blizzard in the lodge owned by John Fallon. John bought Thunder Mountain Lodge because he wanted to be by himself. Spending time with Fiona has him wondering if love might be something he wants more.

#1455 A TOWN CALLED CHRISTMAS • Carrie Alexander

A woman named Merry, a town called Christmas. Both could be just what a lonely Navy pilot who's the recipient of a Dear John letter needs. But Mike Kavanaugh isn't looking for a relationship that lasts beyond the holidays. And how can he ask that of Merry when she's expecting a little bundle in just a few months?

#1456 COMFORT AND JOY • Amy Frazier
Twins

Coming home for Christmas—to stay—is not what Gabriel Brant had in mind. Not when it means he and his twin sons have to live with his father. But Hurricane Katrina left him no choice. And now small-town do-gooder Olivia Marshall wants to heal him. Gabriel doesn't want pity. Love? That's a whole other story.

#1457 THE CHRISTMAS BABY • Eve Gaddy
The Brothers Kincaid

The Bachelor and the Baby could be the title of Brian Kincaid's life story. The perpetual playboy has just gotten custody of a baby boy. In desperation, he hires Faith McClain, a single mother of a baby girl, as his nanny. Could marriage and family life be the next chapter?